Somethi
somet

Bonnie was becom
with the mysteries hiding in the shadows at
Redding Institute.

She sighed and brushed her hands together,
removing the residue of crushed leaves. She
frowned, thinking of Nicholas's words. He'd said
he'd paid with his soul for the opportunity to
work here. What exactly did that mean?

With another sigh of frustration, Bonnie stood
up and brushed off the seat of her jeans. She
turned to start back to the house, then froze as
she heard the sound of a branch snapping. The
sound exploded in the quiet of the woods. A wild,
animal scent assailed her nose—not unpleasant, but
alien to her senses. Slowly she turned and looked
around, the hairs on the back of her neck prickling
as she heard the rumble of a growl....

Carla Cassidy is an award-winning author who has written over thirty-five books for Silhouette. In 1995 she won Best Silhouette Romance from *Romantic Times Magazine* for *Anything for Danny*. In 1998 she also won a Career Achievement Award for Best Innovative Series from *Romantic Times Magazine*.

HEART OF
THE BEAST

CARLA CASSIDY

Published by Silhouette Books
America's Publisher of Contemporary Romance

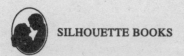

SILHOUETTE BOOKS

ISBN 0-373-51158-2

HEART OF THE BEAST

PROLOGUE

He stood at the window, staring out into the blackness of the night. He wished he could meld into the shadows and disappear like the darkness with the coming of the morning sun.

But of course he couldn't, and so he would remain here in this place that had become both his prison and his sanctuary.

"You didn't eat much dinner."

He turned away from the window and stared at the man who had just entered the room. "I wasn't very hungry."

The newcomer nodded and moved over to the portable bar, where he poured two fingers of Scotch into the bottom of a glass. "Drink?"

The man at the window sat down in a nearby chair and shook his head. "I don't think that's a good idea, do you?"

"I don't think a small drink of good Scotch would cause any problems."

"I'm not willing to take a chance." The man in the chair leaned back and closed his eyes with a weary sigh.

"She should be here sometime tomorrow."

His eyes flew back open and he once again stared

at the man in front of him. "You really are a monster, aren't you?"

The man tossed back his Scotch in two quick gulps, then looked at his seated companion with a humorless smile. "How amusing that you should call me a monster. Don't you think that's a case of the proverbial pot calling the kettle black?"

The man in the chair clenched his hands into fists, fighting against the anger that began as a knot in the pit of his stomach. He knew what anger did to him and he fought against it with every ounce of inner strength he possessed.

But the anger already had a firm grasp, and as it began to unfurl, an insistent prickling sensation attacked his skin. He recognized it immediately, a signal of danger.

"I...must..." He stumbled up from the chair, the prickling sensation now attacking every inch of his skin.

He pushed past the other occupant of the room, aware only of his immediate need. Very soon he would be completely out of control. His sense of self, the essence of his humanity, would slip away. His head pounded with a nauseating intensity, letting him know the end of rational thought swiftly approached.

He stumbled blindly up the stairs and down a long, dark corridor, his breaths coming in short, quick gasps.

I must maintain control. I must maintain control.

He held on to this thought like a reverent child clutching a crucifix.

It wasn't until he was safely locked in the padded room that he stopped fighting the inevitable. He sank down to the floor and waited for the transformation to begin.

CHAPTER ONE

"This is as far as I go." The taxi driver pulled the cab to a stop on the side of the gravel road and shut off the engine.

"I don't understand." Bonnie Redding looked out the window, seeing only the surrounding woods through which they had traveled for the past fifteen minutes. "There must be some mistake. We're out in the middle of nowhere."

The driver took his toothpick out of his mouth and pointed to a set of iron gates nearly obscured by green vines and overgrowth. "There's no mistake. Through the gates and down the lane about a mile, you'll find the institute. Though why you want to is beyond me," he added in an undertone.

"Can't you drive me right to it?" Bonnie asked, not anxious to get out of the cab and walk a mile through the woods at twilight.

"I could, but I won't." He opened his door and stepped out, walking to the trunk, where he removed her large suitcase and set it on the ground.

Bonnie also exited the cab and hurried to where the driver now stood waiting for his fare. She made one last appeal. "I'll pay you an extra ten dollars if you'll drive me the rest of the way."

He threw his toothpick down on the ground and shook his head with a small laugh. "You couldn't pay me enough to drive through them gates." He looked back over to the heavy wrought iron and his smile faded. "There ain't enough money in the world." His face closed up. "That's private property. Nobody's welcome there."

"But I'm an invited guest," Bonnie protested.

"Well, I'm not and I ain't going." He spat on the ground as if to punctuate the finality of his sentence.

He took the money she held out to him and shoved it in his pocket, then looked at her hesitantly. "You sure you want to go in there?" Worry caused the furrows in his brow to deepen.

"Of course. My father lives there," Bonnie explained.

Immediately the worry vanished from his face, replaced by a grim unfriendliness. "Then I'll be on my way." He got back in the taxi and started the engine with a roar. He turned it around and disappeared down the road in a swirl of gravel dust.

With a disgruntled sigh, Bonnie picked up her suitcase and walked to the fence. She shoved on the ornate gate, surprised when it swung open easily without a single creak or groan. Ahead of her lay a well-used lane that, in the distance, seemed to be swallowed up by the woods.

About a mile down the lane.... Terrific, she thought dryly. Hefting her suitcase in one hand, she took off walking, admiring the way the light of dusk played on the autumn leaves.

Bonnie loved autumn. She and her mother had often taken weekend car trips through New England at this time of year. They'd stayed in quaint bed-and-breakfast inns, enjoying the vivid colors the season offered.

There would be no more trips. She had buried her mother three weeks before. Her heart clenched in her chest as a wave of loss swept over her. At the end, death had been a blessing, an end to her mother's pain, but that didn't make Bonnie's heartache and sense of loss any easier to handle.

She shook her head and took a deep breath, pushing the past where it belonged. The past was gone and her future lay ahead, uncertain and unsettling.

She shifted her suitcase from one hand to the other, trudging up the deeply rutted road that would eventually lead her to the Redding Institute, her father's home.

Her father… Her heart beat faster at the thought of finally seeing again the man who'd always held a small part of her heart, but who'd never been more than a minute part of her life.

It had been the death of her mother that had prompted her to come here and find the last remaining family member she had in the world. It had been her mother's death that had made her decide to find the man who had walked out of her life when she was five years old.

She wasn't sure how far she'd walked when she became aware of the silence. It wasn't a normal silence, broken by the rustle of wind-whipped autumn leaves. It wasn't relieved by the scurry of an animal in the underbrush or the call of a bird overhead. It was thick, heavy, oppressive...strange.

She felt a ripple of unease move up her spine. She'd moved deeper into the woods, where the waning evening light didn't penetrate the shadows of approaching nightfall. The trees were gnarled and twisted, attesting to their age by the width of their massive trunks. They seemed to edge closer to the road, as if resenting her very presence.

Her footsteps slowed as her gaze darted first left, then right. A prickly sensation itched in the center of her back, the feeling one always got when being watched.

She whirled around, her eyes narrowed as she searched the lengthening shadows. She saw nobody, yet sensed she was not alone.

"Hello?" she called out. There was no answer, and yet she knew eyes watched her. She knew unseen ears had heard her speak.

She turned and continued walking, faster this time, cursing beneath her breath as she nearly stumbled over an exposed root.

She followed the curve in the road and stopped suddenly, dropping her suitcase and gasping aloud.

All of her attention focused on the structure that rose up from the earth and towered over the treetops. Constructed mostly of massive gray stones and wood blackened with age, it appeared like a medieval fortress built to withstand the ravages of nature and man.

The forest had tried to reclaim its own, sending insidious tendrils and tenacious vines to swallow most of the ground floor of the structure. Giant trees crowded against either side, as if attempting to squeeze out man's existence.

Bonnie shivered. What was her father doing in a place like this? His letters had mentioned that the institute was large enough to accommodate his laboratory and living quarters for his staff. However, she'd expected a modern building surrounded by cozy cottages. This monstrosity looked like something from a horror movie, certainly not like a place where select scientists worked and lived.

"If Norman Bates answers the door, I'm not staying," she muttered, grabbing her suitcase once again and moving forward with hesitant footsteps.

It didn't matter where her father lived. What did matter was her need to connect with him now that her mother was gone.

She walked quickly to the front door, eager to complete the journey that would culminate in a reunion with the man she hadn't seen since she was five years old, a man she really knew only through the memories of her mother and a few treasured ones of her own.

She raised her hand to ring the bell, but hesitated, suddenly worried about what sort of reception she would receive. Her first two letters asking her father if she could come and visit with him had been answered negatively. He was in the middle of an important project, the timing wasn't right, pages of reasons why she shouldn't come. Then suddenly, out of nowhere, she'd received a third letter two days ago, encouraging a visit. She'd been confused, wondering what had prompted his change of mind, but eager to spend some time with him, she had shoved her unease aside and made the arrangements for the trip.

Taking a deep breath, she now rang the bell, hearing the chime echoing deep within. Immediately the heavy door swung open. "May I help you?" The woman was middle-aged, with a face that somehow suggested unyielding strength. Her dark red hair was shot through with gray and pulled back in a bun. The dress she wore was severe in cut, a somber gray in color.

"I'm Bonnie Redding. I believe I'm expected."

"Ah, yes. Please come in." A smile moved the woman's lips upward, but didn't reach the brown of her eyes. She opened the door wider to admit Bonnie into a large foyer. "Your father has been anxiously awaiting your arrival. If you'll wait in the library I'll let him know you are here."

Bonnie nodded, following the woman into a room that, despite the blazing fire in the stone fireplace, offered no warmth or sense of welcome.

"Please make yourself at home and I'll get Dr. Redding." She motioned for Bonnie to have a seat, then left the room, closing the massive double doors behind her.

Alone in the room, Bonnie looked around curiously, trying to orient herself to the strangeness of the place.

The room was large, with thick walls that were adorned with shelf after shelf of books. The books themselves were impressive looking, heavy volumes of scientific facts and theories, the titles alone daunting.

The ceiling was high, the cavernous room making her footsteps echo hollowly as she walked across the wooden floor.

She stood before the fire, welcoming the warmth the blaze offered. There seemed to be a chill surrounding her, and she wasn't sure whether it was an actual physical thing or the manifestation of her anxiety.

She turned as the double doors flew open and a gray-haired man in a white lab coat entered.

"Bonnie." He crossed the room in quick strides, stopping as he came to stand directly before her. "Let me look at you," he said softly, his blue eyes searching her face. "Ah, you're beautiful, the very image of your mother." He reached out and took her hands in his. "I'm so glad you've come."

The words, so long imagined, so desperately yearned for, caused emotion to explode in Bonnie's chest. She'd been so afraid…afraid that somehow, since writing that last letter, he would have changed his mind once again. "I'm glad I'm here, too," she replied, studying him intently.

Funny, she'd always had the impression he was tall, but in reality he was only average height, scarcely taller than her own five foot six.

"Come, we were just about to sit down to dinner. I'll introduce you to my colleagues." She started to pick up her suitcase. "Don't worry about that. Jimmy will get it and take it to your room." He took hold of her elbow and led her from the library, down the hallway and into a formal dining room. Three men were already seated at the table, and they looked up curiously as Bonnie and her father entered.

"Gentlemen, I'd like to introduce my daughter, Bonnie." The men all murmured their greetings. "Bonnie, this is Dr. Bill Taylor, Dr. Jerrod Washington, and Dr. Michael Wellsburn. You'll sort out who's who as time goes on." He smiled at her. "You'll have plenty of time to learn all about these nefarious characters who work with me." He turned to the woman who'd let Bonnie in. She stood in the doorway that apparently led to the kitchen. "Mavis, we'll need another place setting at the table."

"I don't want to be a bother," Bonnie protested.

"Nonsense," her father said briskly. "We would have had a place set but we weren't sure exactly what time to expect you." He moved to the head of the table and gestured for her to sit at his immediate right. There followed a moment of confusion as one of the doctors moved down the table and Mavis prepared a place for Bonnie.

"Where's Nicholas?" Walter Redding's gaze shot to the opposite end of the table, where a place was set, but the chair was empty. He turned and looked at one of the other doctors. "Where is he, Jerrod?"

Jerrod Washington, a gaunt, nearly bald man, flushed crimson. "He went out earlier."

"I thought you were together." The words were spoken softly, in measured tones.

"We were, but the man is like a chameleon out in the woods." His flush deepened. "I can't keep up with him."

Bonnie watched this exchange between her father and his co-worker with interest, slightly unsettled by the tension that suddenly vibrated in the air.

"Well, we may as well get started," Walter said, unfolding his linen napkin and placing it in his lap. He nodded to Mavis, who disappeared back into the kitchen only to return seconds later with a tray of soup bowls and a tureen of steaming liquid.

"Bonnie, what do you think of the Redding Institute?'' Dr. Wellsburn asked as Mavis served their soup.

''From what little I've seen so far, it isn't exactly what I expected,'' she answered, smiling at Mavis as the woman set a bowl of what looked like a thick cheese soup in front of her. ''I had imagined something with a little less character and a lot more chrome and stainless steel,'' she admitted truthfully.

Her father laughed. ''Ah, just because we're a bunch of eggheads doesn't mean we don't appreciate a civilized life-style.''

''Civilized? I could think of other adjectives to describe this particular life-style.''

Everyone turned at the sound of the deep voice. Bonnie felt her breath catch in her throat as she saw the man who stood in—no, *filled*—the doorway. He was younger than the others at the table, probably not older than thirty-five. His hair was the color of midnight, curling slightly over his ears and around the nape of his neck. He had bold, dark eyebrows, high cheekbones that threw shadows on the skin below, a straight, aristocratic nose, and lips that spoke of an innate sensuality. However, it was his eyes that held her, pale silvery eyes that gleamed with the cunning of a wild animal, yet held a melancholy that was strangely compelling.

''Ah, Nicholas, you almost missed the soup.'' Bonnie's father smiled pleasantly.

''I lost track of the time.'' He moved through the

doorway and took the seat at the end of the table. He sat as if he owned the space around the chair and was confident that nobody would intrude on that space. When he looked at Bonnie once again, gone was the trace of melancholy, and instead she saw only a cool speculation. "So, you're Walter's daughter."

Bonnie nodded and offered Nicholas a tentative smile, one he didn't return. With a flush, she stared down at her soup.

"Miss Redding, your father has told us you're a teacher," Dr. Wellsburn said, swiping his mustache daintily with the linen napkin.

"Bonnie, please, and yes, that's right. I teach fifth grade. Although I took a leave of absence this year for personal reasons."

Her father reached over and touched her shoulder lightly. "I was so sorry to hear about your mother."

Bonnie nodded, a spasm of pain convulsing inside as she thought of her mother. That particular sense of loss was still too fresh to share with anyone, even the man her mother had professed to love until her last day. "Anyway," she said, "I've been assured my position back on the teaching staff next fall."

"And do you enjoy your work?" Dr. Wellsburn asked.

As the meal progressed, the conversation remained pleasant and light. But despite the friendly interest of her father and the three doctors, it was Nicholas who unsettled Bonnie.

He didn't speak a word throughout the entire meal, but she felt his gaze lingering on her often. She also noticed that the other men watched him covertly, casting surreptitious glances at him.

What a strange bunch, she thought as Mavis served them dessert, a slice of warm apple pie topped with a scoop of ice cream. The only one who didn't seem odd was her father.

As Mavis set his piece of pie before him, Bonnie noticed that her hand touched the back of his neck. It was a simple touch, yet one that spoke of intimacy, and it was at that moment that Bonnie speculated on the possibility that her father and Mavis were lovers.

A fresh shaft of pain ripped through her, only this time, the pain mingled with anger. How dare he! How dare he indulge in a relationship when his wife, Bonnie's mother, had sacrificed and lived alone, respecting his obsession for science. *"He loves us, Bonnie girl. He just loves his work more."* How many times had Bonnie heard those words from her mother, defending him, upholding his decision to live apart.

"What's the matter, dear?" her father now asked.

Bonnie looked up from where she'd been pushing a bite of the pie from side to side on the plate. "Oh…nothing," she answered. "I guess I'm just a little tired." She gave him a tight smile. "I'm fine, really."

Maybe I'm imagining everything, the strange tension and air of expectancy between the men, she thought. Maybe she was just tired and had imagined the implied intimacy between her father and Mavis. Bonnie's mother had always admonished her to use her intuition less and her head more.

Yet it was difficult to think at all when her gaze moved down the table and locked onto Nicholas. He stared at her, and for a moment it was as if all the surroundings faded away and the room held only the two of them.

The silver orbs of his eyes spoke to her, but it was a language she didn't understand. There was danger there, a threat…a warning. There was also another emotion hiding behind his glittering eyes. Like the surface of a pond at sunset, they offered murky depths and hidden mysteries she didn't understand, ones she wasn't sure she wanted to.

She broke the gaze, looking down at her uneaten pie once again. Her heart beat rapidly in her chest. The man was extremely attractive, but there was an animal-like intensity about him that thoroughly unsettled her.

She looked at her father and smiled. This was why she was here, to learn about the man who had fathered her, to fill the void that had always been inside her due to the lack of his presence in her life. This was what was important, and everything else paled in significance.

''They all seem like nice men,'' she said moments

later, as her father led her up a wide, impressive stairway.

"They are some of the brightest minds this country has to offer, committed men who have given up living normal lives in the pursuit of knowledge."

"What about Nicholas?" she asked casually, running her hand up the smooth wooden banister as they advanced up the carpeted stairs.

"Ah, Nicholas." An enigmatic smile played on his features. "Nicholas Shepherd is brilliant. Unfortunately, there are times I believe his brilliance borders madness." He placed a hand at the small of her back as they reached the top of the stairs. "I think you might find him interesting, although it might be a good idea if you stay a healthy distance from him."

She nodded, having already reached the same conclusion herself. She followed her father down a long, dark corridor.

"We all have our bedrooms here on this floor," he explained. "Mine is here at this end. Nicholas has his quarters at the far end, and the others are in between." He stopped at the door next to his. "I've put you in here." He opened the door and she walked in, pleasantly surprised by the cheeriness of the room.

A fire snapped and popped in the fireplace, casting amber lights on the daisy-laden wallpaper. Bright yellow gauzy curtains hung at the French doors that apparently led out to a balcony, matching the spread on the four-poster bed. The furniture was antique, a dark wood that lent an understated elegance to the room.

"The bath is right through there." He pointed to a doorway next to the closet. "I hope you'll be comfortable in here."

"It's a lovely room," she assured him. She walked over to the fireplace. "It's strange. This place makes me feel like I've somehow stepped back into time."

Walter smiled in understanding. "Yes, in this main part of the house with the fireplaces and antique furnishings, it's easy to imagine one is back in the eighteenth century. When you see the lab, you'll feel like you've stepped into the twenty-first century. The short amount of time we find ourselves away from the lab, we enjoy the simplicity and elegance of this old place."

"Where exactly is the lab?" Bonnie asked curiously.

"In the basement. I'll take you on a complete tour tomorrow." He looked around the room and frowned. "Where are your things? Jimmy should have brought them up by now."

At that moment a young man came through the doorway, lugging Bonnie's suitcase at his side. He was probably no older than fifteen or sixteen, with the kind of face Bonnie had always imagined on Tom Sawyer. Thin faced, covered with freckles and sporting a burst of copper-colored hair, the face held an expression of innocence, an openness and friendliness that immediately made Bonnie smile.

"Jimmy, I was wondering where you were," Walter said, and Bonnie noticed that Jimmy's eyes focused intently on Walter's mouth. Walter turned to Bonnie. "Jimmy is Mavis's son. He's a deaf-mute."

Bonnie approached the young man and held out her hand. "Hi, Jimmy."

He shook her hand and offered her a shy smile, his face reddening in a self-conscious blush.

Walter touched him on the shoulder and pointed to the door. Jimmy immediately dropped Bonnie's hand and left the room.

"Well, I'll leave you now and let you get settled in." He turned to leave.

"Uh...Father?" The title felt alien on Bonnie's lips.

He turned and looked at her curiously.

"I was hoping we'd have a few minutes to talk...just the two of us." There were so many questions she had for him, so many things she wanted to know.

He smiled. "There will be plenty of time for that later. But tonight, I still have work to do in the lab." With a slight nod, he left the room, closing the door behind him.

The moment he was gone, Bonnie moved back over to stand before the fire. She shouldn't feel disappointed. She really hadn't expected a marathon session of auld lang syne on the first night of her arrival.

She moved from the fireplace over to the mirror that hung above the antique dresser. She stared at her reflection, trying to find in her image some vestige of the man who'd just left the room.

Certainly there was no similarity between her own shoulder-length blond hair and her father's steel gray. Her eyes were green, his were blue. Her chin was slightly pointed, his was square. She'd always known that physically she favored her mother, but she was somehow disappointed that she found not a single physical trait she'd inherited from her father.

She turned away from the mirror with a sigh. She picked up her suitcase and opened it on the bed. She'd unpack, take a bath and go to bed. She was tired, not only from the trip from her home in New England to this place in the woods of Arkansas, but also from the past months of stress in caring for her terminally ill mother.

She was pleased to discover that although the plumbing in the bathroom looked horrendously antiquated, steaming-hot water gushed from the tub faucet, and the tub itself was unusually deep and large.

She stayed in the big tub until the water had cooled and the skin on the bottom of her toes was wrinkled and pruned. The long bath was an indulgence she hadn't had in months.

Regardless of the outcome of this trip as it concerned her father, it was good for her to be away from the house where her mother had died. It was good for her to get a chance to reorient herself to real life. She'd been in a sickroom for six long months. It was time for her to live again.

After changing into her nightgown, she turned down the blankets on the bed, then shut off the light. The fire created a golden glow that was somehow comforting.

On impulse, rather than crawling right into bed, she moved to the window and drew the curtains aside. Opening the doors, she stepped out onto the small balcony.

The moon was halved, giving an eerie illumination to the darkness of the woods. The air was cool, caressing her skin and bringing goose bumps to the surface. She wrapped her arms around herself, noting again the utter silence that permeated the area.

Being a city girl, she wondered if perhaps the silence was normal. Yet she knew instinctively that it was not. Surely the woods housed creatures that would scurry through the tangled underbrush. Certainly the trees were home to a variety of birds. She'd never heard a silence so profound, so unnatural.

A branch snapped, the sound exploding out of the quiet like a gunshot in a graveyard. Bonnie's heart banged against her ribs as her gaze sought the cause of the sound.

If the moonlight hadn't been so brilliant, she

wouldn't have seen him at all. As it was, he almost looked like a shadow blending into the darkness cast from one of the nearby trees.

Nicholas Shepherd. What was he doing out in the woods in the darkness of the night? He appeared to be doing nothing, simply standing still as if he had become a permanent part of the surrounding forest.

Brilliance that bordered madness... She remembered her father's words. At that moment he looked up, the moonlight catching in his eyes, reflecting up to her. Yes, there was a madness there, a haunting, tormented madness that both compelled and repelled her.

With a swift intake of breath, she moved back to her room and closed the doors, carefully locking them. She then jerked the curtains tightly closed.

She crawled into bed and pulled the covers up around her neck. Cold...she was suddenly very cold. She closed her eyes, her mind still filled with the vision of his eyes shining up at her.

I'm tired, she told herself. *I'm just tired.*

What was he doing out there in the dark? she wondered, then chided herself. *The man goes out to take a nighttime walk and I imagine all kinds of weird things.* She smiled at her own childishness. Closing her eyes once again, she willed her heartbeats to slow, concentrated on getting her muscles to relax, and within minutes she was sound asleep.

* * *

She awoke with a start. The room was dark, the flames of the fire gone, leaving only embers behind, embers that emitted no light, but glowed like mysterious monster eyes.

She lay unmoving, her heart beating in a rhythm of unease, and wondered what it had been that had pulled her from her pleasant dreams.

Suddenly it came, splitting the night. A masculine cry of such torment, such rage that it made her heart seem to stop cold in her chest. It lasted only a moment. It sounded almost inhuman.

What was it? Who was it? She huddled deeper beneath the blankets, shivering…waiting for morning to come.

CHAPTER TWO

Nightmares. That was what Bonnie told herself the next morning. She had suffered nightmares created from the stress of finally being here at the institute, bad dreams brought on by what her mother had always termed her frenzy-driven imagination.

With the brilliant early morning sunshine filtering through the gauzy curtains, bringing with it a sunshine-scented warmth, it was easy to dismiss the eerie cries of the night before as products of bad dreams and nothing more.

She dressed quickly, abandoning her usual attire of jeans and sweatshirt for a pair of tailored burgundy slacks and a pale pink blouse. She knew she was just being silly. Her father wasn't going to make a judgment call about her character based on her choice of clothing. Still, she didn't want to take any chances. She wanted her father to not only love her because she was his daughter, but also to respect and admire the person she had become.

She checked her reflection one last time, assuring herself that her shoulder-length hair was neatly brushed and her makeup was subtle and natural looking. With a confident smile at her reflection, she turned and left her room.

She saw nobody as she walked down the huge staircase, her footsteps echoing an empty hollowness. *Where is everyone?* she wondered, looking at her wristwatch. It was only a few minutes after seven. Surely somebody was awake in the house besides herself.

Ah, Mavis was obviously awake, she thought, breathing deeply of the scent of fresh-brewed coffee that teased her nose as she entered the dining room. "Hello?" she called softly, smiling as Mavis pushed through the doorway from the kitchen. "Good morning. Am I the first one up?"

"You're the last one up," Mavis replied, motioning Bonnie to have a seat at the table. Bonnie sat down, noticing that there was no warmth, no spark of pleasantness, on the older woman's face. There was only a strained passivity that instantly made Bonnie feel ill at ease. Once again, she noticed the housekeeper was dressed in a somber gray, severely cut dress.

"What can I get you for breakfast?" Mavis asked.

"Oh, nothing. I'm not much of a morning eater. If it's all right, I'll just get myself a cup of coffee." Bonnie started to rise.

"It's my job to get you what you want," Mavis replied, her tone putting Bonnie firmly in her place. She disappeared back into the kitchen and returned a moment later with a cup of steaming coffee. She set it down in front of Bonnie. "If that's all you need, I have work to do in the kitchen.'' She started to leave, but hesitated as Bonnie called after her.

''Where is everyone else?'' Bonnie asked.

''Working. Dr. Redding expects everyone to be down in the labs by six o'clock every morning.''

Bonnie nodded slowly, surprised at how early the days began for the scientists. ''Perhaps when I finish my coffee I'll just go down and look around.''

''You can't do that,'' Mavis retorted sharply, emotion glittering for the first time from her eyes. ''Nobody goes down to the lab without Walter's specific permission.''

''But he's my—''

''I don't care who or what he is to you. The same rules apply to everyone.'' She turned to leave, but not before Bonnie saw a glare of resentment sweep over her face. It was there for only a moment, but savage in its intensity. Its unexpectedness rocked Bonnie like a sharp slap across the face.

''Now what was that all about?'' she muttered to herself as Mavis left the dining room. She sipped her coffee thoughtfully, wondering why the housekeeper would have any reason to resent her.

She remembered that moment the day before when she'd seen the housekeeper's hand linger on her father and suspected the two might be lovers. If it was true, then perhaps Mavis did resent Bonnie's presence here. After all, Bonnie was a reminder that Walter had made a previous commitment, a marriage he'd remained in despite separation and the passing of time.

In truth, Bonnie couldn't help but feel a certain amount of resentment herself as she thought of her father and Mavis together. It seemed so unfair that her father had eased his loneliness in the arms of another woman while his wife had spent years alone, clinging to the memory of the man she had loved and married.

But that's why I'm here, Bonnie reminded herself. She was here to deal with her ambivalent feelings about Walter Redding, fulfill her emotional need to understand him, love him.

She reached for her coffee cup, sloshing some of the liquid on the table as Nicholas Shepherd entered the room.

"Oh, you startled me," she exclaimed, grabbing her napkin to sop up the mess.

"Then you startle very easily," he replied. He went to the doorway of the kitchen and pushed open the door. "Mavis, could I have a cup of coffee?" He walked over to the table and sat down directly across from Bonnie.

"Mavis told me everyone had already gone down to the lab," Bonnie explained.

"I don't keep the same hours as the others," he returned.

She studied him covertly over the top of her cup

as she took another drink, once again struck by his commanding presence.

This morning he wore jeans and a black turtleneck sweater, the sleeves pushed up to expose muscular forearms covered with dark hair. He looked tired, as if he'd had a particularly restless night. His dark hair was unruly and his strong jawline was blurred by a day's growth of whiskers. For some reason, his untidiness lent him an air of vulnerability.

It was only when his strange, moon-slivered eyes met hers that she knew the aura of vulnerability was a mirage. His eyes radiated an electric control, the feeling that he carried within him a tightly coiled spring that might explode at any moment. And Bonnie had an idea that such an explosion would not be pleasant to experience.

Mavis came out of the kitchen and set his cup of coffee before him, backing away from him almost immediately. "Will there be anything else?" she asked, and Bonnie noticed she didn't look directly at Nicholas.

"This is fine," he replied. "I hope you slept well last night," he said to Bonnie when Mavis had escaped back to her kitchen.

"I slept all right," she answered, then added hesitantly, "although I did have a few nightmares."

"Ah, yes, I think most of us here at the institute suffer nightmares of one kind or another."

"Even you?" she asked curiously, finding it impossible to believe that any nightmare would dare intrude on this man's sleep.

He stared at her long and hard, his eyes seeming to reach inside and stroke her soul with icy hands. "Even me, but most of my nightmares occur when I'm not sleeping."

She started to ask him what he meant, but at that moment her father came in. "Ah, I see you're awake," he said to Bonnie, then focused his attention on Nicholas. "I was just on my way up to get you. We've been waiting for you."

Bonnie stood up. "Could I see the lab? I'm really interested to see where you work."

"Perhaps later this morning," he answered. "We're in the middle of some important testing at the moment." He looked at his wristwatch. "I'll take you down and show you around just before lunch. Why don't we meet back here at eleven."

Bonnie nodded, swallowing her initial disappointment. As her father and Nicholas left, Bonnie looked at her watch and sighed. She had a little over three hours to entertain herself.

She looked over at the window where the morning sun beat against the panes with the last gasp of the Indian summer's warmth. It would be a good morning to explore the grounds surrounding the institute, she decided.

She wondered if she should tell somebody she was going out. But who would she tell? Mavis certainly wouldn't care what she did, and her father was too busy to even know she'd gone out.

She left the dining room and headed for the front door, fighting off a small twinge of self-pity. Not for the first time since her mother's death, she was struck by her isolation, her complete aloneness.

You knew it would take time, she chided herself. Despite his filial connection to her, she hadn't really expected her father to immediately gather her into his arms and heart. Still, it would have been nice, she thought wistfully.

She stepped outside, the bright sun warming her face and shoulders, the evocative scent of the forest surrounding her. It was a pungent odor of pine trees and thick moss, of wild flowers and a strange muskiness of unidentified animals. Beneath it all was the subtle smell of decay, of summer's death and autumn's approach.

She started down the nearest narrow path, no particular destination in mind, just enjoying the physical activity of walking. At first, the going was pleasant. The sun was warm on her back and the path was wide and easy to maneuver.

The farther she went away from the house, the thicker the forest became, closing in around her and making it impossible for the sun's rays to reach the ground. The smell of decay intensified, closing in on her like the trees that now crowded in around her.

The trees rattled their leaves as if disturbed by her

very presence, and overhead a bird squawked in dis-
approval as she passed.

The deeper in she walked, the longer and darker
the shadows became and the more twisted and gnarled
the tree trunks were. The ground beneath her feet
grew more rocky, as if soil couldn't exist in the dark
shadows devoid of sun.

She paused a moment, leaning against one of the
ancient trees, remembering her walk in from the main
road the day before and the taxi driver's refusal to
enter through the ornate iron gates.

She thought about that strange instant when she'd
felt somebody's gaze lingering on her, had the feeling
that some malevolent force watched her approach.

She now shivered, deciding to turn around and
head back toward the house. There was a feeling here
in the forest that menaced, a sense that something
wasn't quite as it should be.

It wasn't until she broke back into the sunlight that
the feeling dissipated and she smiled at her own silliness. Apparently the nightmares that had haunted
her sleep had had a lingering effect on her this morning.

As she approached the house once again she
paused, studying the enormous structure with something close to awe. It was an anomaly, seeming to
grow out of the forest floor like a foreign entity. How
had her father come to live and work here? Who
owned the place? So many questions to be answered.

"All in time," she told herself, following a well-worn path that led around to the back of the house.

Here the tangled overgrowth was less intense, and she could tell that at one time the area had sported a grass lawn and flower beds. However, the lawn now grew wild and free, tickling her ankles and thrusting thorny brambles onto her pant legs.

Ahead she saw the crumbling remains of a large birdbath, the basin now cracked and broken, unable to hold water. Around the base were the remnants of a flower garden, the flowers long gone and the ground now choked with weeds.

There was one small area where the weeds had been pulled and the dark earth freshly turned. It was as if someone had made a feeble attempt to fight against the overwhelming neglect.

She turned to leave, then paused, spotting an area in the distance where the grass was noticeably shorter, thinner, and the ground slightly depressed. Curious, she walked over and was surprised to see that it was a grave. Very little grass covered the area, attesting to the fact that it was not an old grave, but rather one that had been dug in recent months. Weeds grew profusely, nearly obscuring the bronze marker.

Bonnie squatted down on her haunches, pulling at the weeds, curious to see what was written on the plaque.

"'Dr. Jonathon Dennison,'" she read aloud, wondering how the man had died, why he was buried out here in the isolated area. According to the dates on the marker, he'd died a scant four months before.

She sat down on her bottom, continuing the task of pulling at the tenacious weeds that decorated the small tomb marking. With the memory of her mother's funeral so fresh in her mind, it seemed particularly sad for this stranger's grave to be neglected and overgrown, as if he were not only dead, but also quickly forgotten.

She didn't know how long she had worked when she got that same feeling she'd had when walking in the day before...the feeling of being watched. For a moment the light breeze that had been caressing her paused, seemingly holding its breath in anticipation.

She raised her head and looked around. She saw nothing, but felt an electric tension surrounding her, raising the hairs on her arms in unconscious wariness.

Her heart fluttered in her chest as a flock of birds suddenly exploded out of the trees, as if seeking safety in the blue sky above. The frantic sound of their beating wings seemed to echo within her veins as a loud thrashing resounded from the thick woods nearby.

Bonnie's gaze sought the source of the noise, her eyes widening as the crashing grew closer. If it was an animal, it was a large one. She scrambled to her feet, poised to flee, her heartbeat thudding loudly in her ears. Her muscles tensed, ready to run as Jimmy broke through the brush.

Relief whooshed out of Bonnie on a sigh. "Jimmy, you scared me half to death," she exclaimed, then remembered the boy was hearing impaired. Knowing that he'd read her father's lips the day before, she waited until he approached closer, then raised her hand in greeting. "Hi, Jimmy."

He returned her gesture, his grin widening.

"What are you doing out here?" she asked, bending down again.

He shrugged and gestured to the sun.

"Oh yes, it's a nice day to be outside," she agreed. She watched as he walked around to the other side of the grave. With a shy smile, he sat down and began pulling the weeds that Bonnie couldn't reach.

As they worked, she was aware of his gaze lingering on her, and each time she met his glance his face flushed with a fierce blush.

When they were finished, Jimmy ran his hand slowly across the bronze plaque, sadness swallowing up his happy countenance.

"Did you know him?" Bonnie asked softly. Jimmy hesitated a moment, then slowly nodded his head. His eyes radiated a pain of loss that pierced through to Bonnie's own heart. She reached out and took his hand in hers. "He was your friend?"

Again there was a slight hesitation before he nodded. Bonnie squeezed his hands in sympathy. "I'm sorry. I know how difficult it is to lose somebody you care about."

Jimmy nodded once again, his eyes communicating his inner emotion. He offered her a shy, grateful smile as he removed his hand from hers.

It seemed somehow fitting that Jimmy had an open, revealing face and eyes that expressed what was in his thoughts. It was as if fate, having chosen to take away his auditory and oral abilities, decided to bless him with expressive features that said what he needed to say.

Bonnie looked at her wristwatch, surprised to see that it was almost ten o'clock. She stood up and brushed off the seat of her pants, smiling as Jimmy also rose. "I'm going back inside," she told him. "Are you coming, too?"

He shook his head and pulled a small garden spade out of his back pocket, then gestured to the old flower bed surrounding the crumbling birdbath.

"Oh, so you're the one who's begun working there." She smiled at him warmly. "Are you going to plant new flowers?" He nodded. "That's nice, Jimmy. If you prepare it all now, by next spring you can have the whole garden blooming."

The boy blushed, the red creeping up his face to decorate the tips of his ears.

Bonnie smiled and waved goodbye. Just before she walked around the side of the house, she turned back and looked at him. He worked diligently in the flower bed, the sun stroking the brilliant red of his hair.

He was a nice kid, she thought as she walked

around the side of the enormous house. It must get lonely for him out here, stuck with a bunch of scientists in the middle of the woods. She wondered if he had any friends in the nearby town of Hollow Rock. Did he go to school? Why didn't he use sign language?

She had just rounded the side of the house when a scream shot through the air. The scream from her nightmares…raw, intense, causing her heart to crash against her ribs.

It was impossible to discern if the cry was male or female, human or inhuman. It wasn't a sound of pain; rather it was a cry of raging torment, of emotion so raw it ached inside her.

She froze, unable to move as it sounded again, seeming to surround her, infuse her. It bounced off the woods behind her, echoed through the tops of the trees, resounded in the massive stones of the house so that there was no way to guess from where it came.

It stopped as suddenly as it had began, leaving behind a strange silence that engulfed the entire area. It was as if every creature, great and small, who lived in the woods, held its breath and cowered silently beneath the weight of the tormented cry.

Bonnie's initial paralysis broke, and she ran through the front door, into the safety of the house. She raced into the dining room where Mavis was busy setting the table for lunch. "Did you hear it?" she asked the older woman breathlessly.

Mavis paused, looking at her blankly.

"The scream," Bonnie prompted. "I was outside and there was a horrible scream."

Mavis began folding a stack of linen napkins, her face a mask of neutrality. "You probably heard a coyote or a bear. The woods are full of animals."

"But it didn't sound like an animal," Bonnie exclaimed, wrapping her arms around herself to ward off an imminent chill as she thought about the strange, eerie cry. "I didn't think coyotes howled during the day."

"Coyotes howl whenever they want to—they don't need a special reason or time."

Bonnie waited for the housekeeper to say more, but her attention was once again on the task of setting the table. The chill Bonnie had been fighting against now engulfed her as she turned and headed upstairs to her room.

A coyote or a bear… She thought about Mavis's explanation. It seemed logical. It made sense. But as she thought about the raw emotion, the tortured rage contained in the cry, she knew with a gut-wrenching certainty that it had been no coyote. It had been no animal at all. The frightening thing was that it also seemed impossible that the sound had emanated from a human being. So what did that leave? she wondered, shivering once again as a cold fear slowly uncoiled in the pit of her stomach.

* * *

"This is like something from a science-fiction movie," Bonnie exclaimed to her father as he led her around the laboratory.

Descending the stairs into the basement of the old house had been like entering a different world. Downstairs there was no hint of the ancient age of the house. The walls were some sort of gleaming white fiberglass, the lighting brilliant as it reflected off the stainless-steel tables and state-of-the-art equipment.

The scientists were at work, most of them in front of computer monitors. Bonnie felt the fascination of a neophyte among experts in an alien world. The smattering of scientific knowledge she possessed was limited to what she needed to know to teach the fifth-graders in her classroom.

However, she did possess a hunger to know about this world that had stolen her father away from her. "What exactly are you working on?" she asked him.

"We've managed to isolate several links in the chain of DNA structure. We're in the process of manipulating them in an effort to discourage negative inherited characteristics." Walter's face seemed to light from within as he showed her the various pieces of equipment, explaining the techniques and uses of each.

Although Bonnie understood little of what he was explaining to her, for the first time since arriving she felt as if he was reaching out to her, trying to connect with her in the only way he knew how. And so she listened, understanding little, but admiring the nobility of their cause, their intense dedication to their work.

It wasn't until her father had finished his explanation, that Bonnie noticed a closed door that obviously led to an area she hadn't seen. "What's in here?" she asked, reaching out for the doorknob but pausing as her father stopped her.

"That's my personal office and lab. Nobody goes in there except me." Walter took her elbow and smiled. "Now, shall we go upstairs? It's time for lunch."

As Bonnie and her father started upstairs, the other men followed. "Where's Dr. Shepherd?" Bonnie asked. The dark, attractive man had been conspicuously absent from the lab area.

"Nicholas had a restless night last night and a bad morning. He's retired to his rooms," Walter explained as they entered the dining room. "I noticed you had coffee with him this morning. I hope he was pleasant enough?"

Pleasant? That wasn't exactly the way Bonnie would have described Nicholas Shepherd's personality. "He was fine," she told her father. "I scarcely had a chance to talk to him at all."

Walter nodded as if in satisfaction. "My dear, I must admit, Nicholas is a fascinating man. The man is a brilliant scientist, but as it is with most geniuses, his emotional makeup and humanity is slightly underdeveloped.'' He looked at her speculatively. ''Still, I'm sure he could use a friend.'' He patted Bonnie's arm, sending a welcome warmth spreading through her. ''You might want to keep that in mind. Anyway, enough talk about Nicholas. I'm hungry—how about you?''

Bonnie nodded, still warmed by her father's attention, intrigued by thoughts of becoming friends with the darkly handsome Nicholas. Her positive feelings lasted throughout lunch, which consisted of hot roast beef sandwiches. Mavis might be an old sourpuss in the personality department, Bonnie thought, but the woman definitely knew how to cook.

As they ate, the conversation once again revolved around their work, with words and terms that made Bonnie feel as if they were all speaking a foreign language she couldn't understand. Still, she didn't mind. The warmth of her father's attention toward her was like a balm on her wounded, grieving spirit, and she hoped this was the beginning of a closer relationship with the man who was her last living relative.

''What was this place before you came here?'' Bonnie asked her father as they all finished the meal.

''I don't know the entire history of the house, but from what I do know it has had a varied, rather dark past,'' Walter explained. ''It was built in the late 1800s by a man named Richard Ravenscrest. He built it as a tribute to his beautiful young wife. They only lived here for about a month when she wandered off the grounds and got lost in one of the nearby caves. She was never found, and Richard eventually went quite mad.''

"Oh, how sad," Bonnie exclaimed.

"Richard had no family, so when he died, the house sat empty for years and years. In the 1920s the place was taken over by the state and turned into an insane asylum." He paused a moment as Mavis reached across him to retrieve his now-empty plate. "Unfortunately," he continued as she cleared the other dishes, "as the years went by, Ravenscrest became home to the most hopeless cases of mental illness. It remained a snake pit of sorts until the late 1960s, when the federal government intervened. The patients were placed in more up-to-date institutions, and they decided because of the isolation, this was a perfect place for me to work and do research. Thus, it is now the Redding Institute."

Bonnie sighed and looked around her. "Imagine if these walls could talk, all the stories they could tell." She shivered, unsure if she'd want to hear what the walls would say.

"Indeed." Walter smiled with amusement. "Some probably best left as secrets forever."

"So you've been here all these years?" Bonnie asked.

Her father nodded. "Mavis and I are the only ones who have been here since the beginning. Nicholas has been here for the past eight months." He smiled at the other men at the table. "These men joined me two months ago. The staff has changed over the years, but I believe I have finally assembled together the gifted minds that will achieve the success we've sought for so long."

The other men at the table beamed at Walter. "We are privileged to be working with a man like your father," Dr. Wellsburn, the mustached scientist, said.

Bonnie nodded, handing Mavis the half-emptied gravy boat from the center of the table. "Oh, I almost forgot." Bonnie looked at her father. "I was just wondering, who was Jonathon Dennison?"

The gravy boat suddenly slid from Mavis's hands to the floor, where it thunked against the rug, spilling the remaining gravy as it skittered to a halt. "Oh, how clumsy of me," she exclaimed, bending down to clean up the mess.

But as Bonnie watched the woman move to clean the spilled gravy, she felt a shiver of apprehension trek up her spine. For just a moment, as Bonnie mentioned Jonathon Dennison's name, Mavis's eyes had radiated a threatening anger, and beneath that, a cold, stark fear.

CHAPTER THREE

"Now, where were we?" Walter asked when the mess had been cleaned up and Mavis had retreated once again to the kitchen.

"I had asked about Jonathon Dennison," Bonnie reminded him.

"Ah, yes, poor Jonathon." Walter meticulously rearranged his napkin on his lap. "Jonathon was a colleague, a friend of mine. He was one of the original staff members when we first opened the labs. He died several months ago, a massive heart attack."

"Why is he buried in the back?"

Walter shrugged his shoulders. "Jonathon didn't have any family. He often talked about the fact that Mavis and I were the only family he cared about, the institute the only place he'd ever felt at home. We thought it fitting that he be laid to rest here, in the old cemetery."

Bonnie nodded, confused by the reasonableness of her father's answer in comparison to Mavis's reaction at the mention of the dead scientist's name. Had it been mere clumsiness that had caused her to drop the gravy boat? Bonnie frowned. Had she only imagined that look of anger and fear on the housekeeper's face? She could almost hear her mother's voice admonishing her. *"There you go again, Bonnie Sue, overworking that imagination of yours."*

She looked around the table, studying the faces of her father's co-workers. None of them seemed to be unduly disturbed by the mention of Jonathon's name. Quit looking for trouble where there is none, she admonished herself.

Once again the conversation returned to lab tests and procedures, and Bonnie's mind drifted to the man who was absent from the group.

Despite her father's negative comments concerning the man, she couldn't help but admit she found something intriguing about Dr. Nicholas Shepherd. Perhaps it had something to do with the shadows that flitted across his moon-colored eyes, shadows as deep and impenetrable as the darkness of night.

There was an edge to him that both repelled and drew her, a soft voice of danger that whispered in her ear. The fact that her father had initially cautioned her away from the man seemed only to heighten her attraction to him. She smiled at this thought.... A latent perverse streak of rebellion? Surely, at twenty-five, she was too old for such nonsense. Still, she had to admit, there was a touch of the forbidden-fruit syndrome at work here. But, she consoled herself, it really wasn't forbidden fruit. Her father had indicated that the man could use a friend.

"Well, gentlemen," Walter said as he stood up. "I believe it's time for us to get back to work."

"Uh, Father..." Bonnie hesitated, the intimate appellation feeling strange on her lips. "I was wondering if perhaps this evening after dinner we could spend some time together...talk about mother and... uh...things."

"We'll see what the evening brings," Walter said. He smiled distantly, then motioned for the men to follow him back down the stairs to the lab.

Bonnie remained seated at the table in the large dining room with only the muted sounds of dishes being washed in the kitchen to break the silence.

She felt cold, but knew it wasn't a physical manifestation, but rather a response to the emotional environment that surrounded her. It was cold and impersonal. After the years of loving warmth from her mother, her father's distance and lack of real emotion was a jolt.

"Tonight," she murmured, the word a promise to herself. This evening surely she and her father would have a chance to really talk, speak of the past, contemplate their future relationship.

She placed her napkin next to her plate, looking up as Mavis entered the dining room again carrying a tray apparently to be used to gather the last of the dirty dishes.

Bonnie stifled the impulse to help the woman, knowing any attempt to help with the work would only be met with resentment. "The roast beef was delicious," she observed pleasantly.

Mavis merely grunted, busying herself picking up the remaining dishes. Bonnie watched her for a moment or two, frustration niggling at her as she wondered how to break through the older woman's icy composure. "So, you've been here since the very beginning," Bonnie said lightly.

"For nearly twenty years the institute has been my home," Mavis returned.

"So you must have known Jonathon Dennison."

This time there was no reaction on Mavis's face. She looked at Bonnie dispassionately. "Jonathon was Jimmy's father."

"Oh, Mavis, I'm so sorry," Bonnie replied, realizing now what had caused the woman to drop the gravy boat at the mention of the name. Perhaps this also explained the woman's somber clothes. She was still in mourning, Bonnie thought sympathetically.

"No need to waste sorrow on the dead. The ones left behind—the living—those are the ones who need sorrow." She sighed, then compressed her thin lips tightly. "There's work to be done," she finally said, ignoring Bonnie as she filled the tray and disappeared back into the kitchen.

Bonnie sat for a moment or two longer, then headed up to her room, her thoughts still on Mavis, on Jimmy and on the man who now rested out back in the grave.

Poor Jimmy. No wonder his face had reflected such

grief when she'd asked him about the grave and if the deceased was a friend.

Bonnie's heart expanded with empathy for the young man. She knew very well how it felt to lose a parent, and she was more determined than ever to gain some sort of understanding and knowledge of the man who was her father. With her mother so recently gone, and with a new enlightenment about the brevity of life, it seemed more important than ever that she fulfill her need to know Walter Redding.

With a heavy sigh, she started the water in the tub, deciding there was no better way to wile away her time alone than a long, luxurious bubble bath.

Minutes later she lay her head back against the cool porcelain of the deep tub, allowing the fragrant water to envelop her.

The last several months of her mother's life had been incredibly difficult ones for Bonnie. She not only had the emotionally wrenching experience of watching her mother die, but also the physical demands of nursing her twenty-four hours a day.

The cancer had not been kind, the treatment almost as devastating, and although she should have been in the hospital, her mother had insisted she wanted to die at home. So Bonnie had become nurse and caretaker, every day seeing her mother grow weaker, every hour the scent of death in the house more pervasive. Each day had been physically demanding, emotionally draining, as Bonnie gave so much of herself to her loving task.

Now, although the loss of her mother was still fresh, this time alone to indulge in something as simple as a long bath was healing.

She must have dozed off, for when she awoke the water surrounding her was tepid and the bubbles dissipated. She got out and dried off, then slipped on her terry-cloth robe. She picked up her wristwatch, noting that it was only a few minutes after two. It would still be hours until dinnertime.

She walked over to the French doors, opening them and stepping out onto the balcony. She hadn't been able to tell last night in the darkness, but now she could see that the balcony was situated so that it overlooked the back grounds.

She could see the old flower bed where Jimmy had been working, the crumbling birdbath, and beyond that the grave of Jonathon Dennison. It had been someplace in this area that she had seen Nicholas the night before. What had he been doing standing in the darkness near the woods?

In the night, the tangled vegetation of the copse had looked ominous and menacing. But now, with the afternoon sunshine stroking the area in brilliance, with the gentle, warm breeze conducting the leaves in a symphony of rustling, there was a primal beauty that soothed and seduced.

She raised her face to the sunshine, breathed deeply

of the warm air. Perhaps her father was smart to have his lab in this place, where it would be easy to regain a communion with the earth after long hours in the sterile lab.

She smiled when Jimmy suddenly appeared, coming out of the house, his hair gleaming like a copper kettle in the sunshine. He walked across the backyard, his gait the happy, carefree walk of youth. He sat down by the flower bed, pulled out his spade and set to work. The sun reflected off the spade as he adeptly maneuvered it to turn over the soil.

He'd worked for only a moment or two when his head suddenly lifted and he looked around, as if he sensed her gaze on him. He spotted her and waved, the friendliness of his gesture filling her heart with an answering warmth. She waved back, then turned and went back into the room.

Jimmy was the only one who seemed pleased at her presence here, she thought, then scolded herself. Of course her father was pleased she was here; he just wasn't a man who wore his emotions easily.

She grabbed a book she'd packed in her overnight case and lay down on the bed. There was nothing like a good mystery novel to help pass time.

"I'm afraid, my dear, that you'll find me a pitiful host, but we are in the middle of the culmination of some essential tests," Walter explained to Bonnie later that evening as they all sat at the dinner table.

"I trust you were able to entertain yourself this afternoon?"

Bonnie nodded. "I read a couple chapters of a mystery novel I brought with me."

"You're welcome to read anything you find in the library," he offered.

"There's a wonderful poetry collection," Jerrod Washington offered, surprising Bonnie enormously. The bald, emaciated man didn't look like the type who would enjoy poetry. But he'd obviously made the same mistake about her reading preference, for she couldn't abide reading the stuff. Still, she nodded her thanks for his suggestion.

She refocused her attention to the food on her plate. Once again, she was impressed by the meal. Mavis had cooked a savory fish, flavored with lemon and butter. Boiled new potatoes, creamy coleslaw and thick sweet corn bread completed the feast.

Nicholas was again absent from the table. In fact, Bonnie had seen nothing of the man since their brief conversation early that morning. She knew Nicholas's quarters were just down the hallway from her own room, but she hadn't heard a sound from there all afternoon. She hoped he wasn't ill, but she didn't feel comfortable asking her father about him.

They had just about finished the meal when the dining room door flew open, hitting the wall behind it with a bang. Jimmy, his blue eyes widened in horror, raced to Walter's side, his hands flailing wildly as his mouth worked soundlessly to communicate.

"Jimmy, what's wrong?" Walter asked, a touch of impatience in his tone as the boy grabbed his hand and tugged him out of his seat.

Mavis came into the dining room, worry furrowing her brow. "You'd better go with him. Something is wrong," she exclaimed.

Walter allowed Jimmy to pull him toward the front door, the other men also getting up and going with them. Bonnie followed behind them all, wondering what on earth Jimmy was so upset about.

They all walked outside, where dark night clouds had stolen the last gasp of day, and for the first time Bonnie noticed that Jimmy held a flashlight.

He turned it on and focused the small beam on the ground near the base of an enormous tree. There, lying in the tall grass, was the body of a dead raccoon. Bonnie gasped, closing her eyes momentarily against the grotesque sight.

"Good God, Jimmy, you dragged us away from our evening meal because of a dead animal?" Walter snapped impatiently. "It was probably sick, or wounded."

Jimmy shook his head fiercely and with the tip of his shoe rolled the animal over. The belly of the raccoon had been viciously ripped open, its entrails pulled from its body. Nausea rose in Bonnie's throat and she whirled away from the horrid sight.

"Survival of the fittest," Walter explained. "A coyote must have gotten it."

"What's going on?" Nicholas's deep voice came from the doorway of the house. As he walked toward where they all stood, the other men stepped aside, allowing him to see the raccoon.

Bonnie was suddenly aware of a crackling tension in the air. Everyone's attention was focused on Nicholas, and Bonnie found her own gaze riveted to him.

With his dark hair, he appeared to blend in with the shadowy night, but the moon overhead seemed to seek him out, illuminating his face in a ghostly light.

He studied the dead animal for a long moment, his strange eyes glittering with an unnatural brightness. A knot formed in his jaw, and his hands clenched and unclenched at his sides. Without saying a word, he whirled around and stalked back into the house, taking with him the strange, taut force that had surrounded them for a moment.

"Bury it," Walter instructed Jimmy, then turned to the rest of them. "Shall we go back inside and finish our meal?"

Once back at the table, Bonnie discovered her appetite was gone, vanquished by the obscene sight of the mutilated animal. The other men were also unnaturally silent, picking at their food with disinterest. Her father was the only one who seemed undisturbed. He finished his meal and pushed back his plate, emitting a satisfied grunt. "As usual, Mavis quite outdid herself,'' he observed. "The only thing lacking at the moment is a nice glass of brandy." He looked around the table. "Would anyone like to join me in the library?"

Bonnie held her breath as each of the others begged off, pleading exhaustion and an eagerness to retire to their rooms. "I'd love a glass of brandy," she said, thinking it would be a perfect time for an intimate chat between her father and herself.

She followed Walter into the library, where logs had been laid in the fireplace, awaiting only the touch of a match to fire them to life. "Why don't you pour our drinks while I get the fire going," he suggested, gesturing to the portable bar in the corner. She nodded, finding the decanter of brandy and two snifters.

"There's only one complaint I have about this mausoleum," her father continued as he worked to light the logs. "These old stone walls retain so much dampness. But then, I love a crackling fire, don't you?" He brushed his hands together, satisfied as the kindling flamed beneath the thick logs. "There we are," he said, smiling as he took his brandy snifter from her. He motioned her into one of the high-backed wing chairs, sitting down across from her. He took a swallow of the amber liquid, then leaned his head back and closed his eyes, a deep sigh escaping his lips.

Bonnie sipped her drink, the warmth of the mellow liquid sliding down her throat and exploding in the pit of her stomach. She took the opportunity to study her father in his unguarded moment, her gaze examining each minute detail of his face. She had a very vague memory of how he had once looked…his hair dark, his face unlined, so tall and commanding. Although there was still something commanding about him, there was little vestige left of the man her memory retained. His face was lined with time's passage, jarring with the mental picture she had of a younger, more handsome man.

Memories were strange, she thought. It was amazing what pieces of the past the mind decided to retain and turn into treasured remembrances. They often didn't make sense, but were just there, ingrained in the psyche for eternity.

She vaguely remembered a picnic, her father cooking hamburgers and feeding hot dogs to a white mutt. She could envision him shaving in front of a big mirror, reaching out and placing a dollop of cream on the end of her nose. None of her memories had a beginning or an end, they were only isolated moments frozen in time.

She had a sudden desire to reach out and stroke away the lines of his face, to see if she could evoke the smile, the laughter that had been a guarded piece of her past.

He sat so still that she began to wonder if he'd fallen asleep. She was just about to call his name when he opened his eyes and took another sip of his brandy. "It's nice to see that you know the value of silence," he observed. "I never could abide a chatty female."

"Is that why you left Mother?" The question came out of her unbidden. She immediately flushed and bit her bottom lip. "I'm sorry. I guess that's really none of my business."

"You're right, it's not," he agreed, his eyes an arctic blue. "What happened years ago was between your mother and me. The decisions we made at the time were inevitable." He heaved an impatient sigh. "The past is dead, gone. There's no need to be carrions and try to pick it apart."

"I know," Bonnie replied. She leaned forward in the chair. "It's just that she loved you so much. Even though you were gone, she never stopped loving you." She paused a moment and took another sip of the liquor, needing its warmth, wanting its false courage. "At the end, Mother was pretty delirious from the pain and all the drugs. But minutes before she died, she sat straight up in the bed, held out her hand and smiled. She said you were there, waiting for her, that finally you would be together forever. I...I'm sorry." She broke off, swiping at an errant tear that streaked unexpectedly down her cheek.

Walter downed the last of his brandy and stood up, his expression tense. "I must get back to the lab." With an abruptness that startled her, he left the room.

"Father?" she called after him, but he didn't turn

around, didn't even acknowledge that he heard her. "Damn," she muttered, cursing her own stupidity.

She'd pushed too hard, made a mistake in telling him of her mother's last moments. Obviously it had been too much for him.

She sighed and got up to pour herself a bit more brandy, then walked over to the door that opened up onto a small patio.

Carrying her drink outside, she leaned against the wooden railing that partially enclosed the concrete square. The night air immediately settled around her, chilly but not uncomfortable. The surrounding trees were starkly silhouetted by the moonlight overhead, lending an eerie, surreal aura to the grounds. A vaporous mist hung among the trees, obscuring visibility in the distance.

She sipped her drink, her thoughts pulled back to the unsettling sight of the mutilated raccoon. A coyote? A bear? Perhaps. But she'd always had the idea that animals killed each other only for food. So why was the raccoon not eaten? It was as if something vicious, something evil, had torn it apart just for the sheer pleasure of the act.

She shivered, grateful for the internal warmth of the smooth brandy. She would stay out here only long enough to finish her drink. Although she was relatively secure in the knowledge that no wild animal would venture this close to the house, there was something here that also made her believe that the orderly rules of nature no longer applied.

Nicholas Shepherd watched her from his place nearby in the shadowed darkness beneath a large oak tree. He could smell her scent, a spicy fragrance that was sensuous and provocative. He'd noticed it that morning in the dining room and had been surprised by his immediate reaction to it. It had been a long time since he'd smelled a woman, caressed her softness.

His eyes now narrowed as he watched her sipping a drink, seeming to study the night that surrounded her. She was lovely, with the glow of the moon stroking her blond hair with pale fingers.

Although he couldn't see them now, he thought of the green depths of her eyes. In them he had sensed a goodness of spirit, an innocence in her soul. But he wondered if that goodness could be tainted and her innocence perverted into something ugly.

Yes, she was lovely, but it was a loveliness he knew had the ability to seduce him into madness and her to her death.

Damn the man for orchestrating this experiment of ungodliness. Damn him for agreeing to let her come here.

Nicholas knew he should stay away from her, knew he placed her in enormous danger with his proximity. He thought of the dead raccoon, one of the forest innocents killed by the evil spawned by the devil himself.

If he was smart he would stay as far away from Bonnie Redding as possible, keep her isolated from the sickness that tortured his soul. He fought against the vision of her beauty ripped apart, her luminous eyes glazed in death.

He took a step toward the patio, his lips curving upward in a smile of self-derision. Yes, if he was smart he would stay away from her. But he knew that despite his incredible IQ, there were times when he just wasn't very smart.

"The night is beautiful, isn't it."

Bonnie gasped and twirled around at the sound of the deep voice so near to where she stood. Nicholas stepped out of the night mist, walking onto the patio with the stealth of a wild animal.

"Geez, you scared me half to death," she exclaimed, her brandy sloshing over the edge of the glass as he moved to stand next to her.

"You scare easily," he observed.

"Perhaps," she agreed with a smile. "My mother always said I was the type of child who imagined monsters in the closet." She took a step away from him, finding his presence somewhat disturbing. There was something intensely elemental about him, a primitive maleness that drew her to him, yet caused an anxious beat to her heart.

"Maybe the monsters weren't just imagined. Maybe they were really there." He smiled at her, a half quirk of his sensual lips that radiated no warmth, but rather a weary cynicism.

Bonnie laughed. "Now you're trying to give me more nightmares." She took a sip of her brandy and once again leaned against the wooden railing. "The night is beautiful," she said, agreeing with his original statement, her breath catching as he moved to stand so close to her that his broad shoulder touched hers. His scent surrounded her, the smell of the forest, the odor of wildness.

"I like the night. It comforts me."

This confession didn't surprise her. Yes, she would have guessed that he was a man who liked the night, felt comfortable dwelling in the shadows of darkness. "Perhaps you like the night because it makes a good place to hide." She tilted her head and looked at him, wondering where on earth the thought had come from.

This time his smile reached both corners of his mouth and his eyes gleamed like polished silver swords. "I don't need to hide from anything or anyone. It's others who hide from me."

"Why?" she asked, unsure if she really wanted an answer. This was the strangest conversation she'd ever had—and somehow, the most exciting.

He shrugged and stared out into the fog that had

wrapped around them, as if trying to isolate them from the rest of the world.

For a long moment neither of them spoke. The silence grew and thickened like the fog. "Do you believe in evil?" he asked suddenly.

She looked at him in surprise. "Evil?" She contemplated the word, sensing he didn't want a flippant answer, but truly needed her opinion. "Yes, I suppose I believe in evil." She looked out at the fog-shrouded world. "I think there's a constant struggle between the powers of good and evil. But I think it's an internal fight in man's heart. What about you?" she finished curiously, looking back up at him.

He eyed her intently, standing so close to her that she could feel the warm heat of his breath, feel the tension that radiated from his body. "Don't you feel it?" he asked, his voice ominously soft. "Evil lives here. Evil has found a home here at the Redding Institute."

Before Bonnie had a chance to reply, he turned and walked away, disappearing into the ghostly mist of the night.

CHAPTER FOUR

"**J**immy is going into town this morning," Mavis announced as she poured Bonnie a third cup of coffee the next morning. "He wondered if you'd want to go with him." She said the words grudgingly, as if she thought it a poor idea for her son to be in Bonnie's company.

"Oh, I'd love to go," Bonnie replied, as much to irritate the dour old woman as anything. She wasn't accustomed to such unwarranted antipathy. "How soon is he leaving?"

"He's waiting for you out in the garage."

Bonnie downed her coffee in three quick gulps and stood up. "Uh...where's the garage?"

"On the west side of the house, down the hill a ways. Just follow the road," Mavis responded, picking up Bonnie's coffee cup and disappearing into the kitchen.

"Follow the road, indeed," Bonnie muttered minutes later as she trudged down the dirt ruts that were little more than cow paths in the ground. Still, it was a beautiful fall morning, rife with the scents of autumn's perfume.

She'd always believed that she and her mother were seeing the best fall foliage when they traveled through the Connecticut countryside on their weekend trips, but the brilliance of the leaf canopies overhead could rival the New England trees on their best day.

As she walked a little farther, her admiration of the landscape faded. Trees hugged oppressively close to the car tracks, blocking the sunlight that moments before had shone so brightly.

She hugged her purse tighter against her chest, fighting off a wave of sudden paranoia. What was it about this place that made her feel as if she were being watched? It was nothing more than a prickly sensation racing up her spine, but it was so intense it forced her gaze to seek the underbrush and tangled weeds around her, seeking something—anything—that would explain the strange disquiet that swooped down around her. It was as if an omnipotent force watched her, studied her every movement.

She breathed a sigh of relief as she saw the wooden structure of the garage ahead. The entire building tilted slightly to one side, as if advanced age had made it tired. It was obvious that any money spent on renovating had been confined to the house and hadn't included this outbuilding.

"Hello?" she called out hesitantly as she entered the dark yawn of the opened garage door. She shook her head, realizing Jimmy wouldn't hear her call. She walked around the rusted red pickup truck, hoping it wasn't their transportation to town, and spied Jimmy sitting at a workbench.

His back was to her and she approached him hesitantly, not wanting to frighten him with her presence. But before she reached him he twirled around, as if a sixth sense had told him she was there. He grinned, a smile lifting his lips as he saw her. He raised a hand in greeting and she returned the gesture.

"How did you know I was here?" she asked him curiously.

He smiled sheepishly and pointed to his nose, then took a deep breath.

"You smelled me?" she asked incredulously. He nodded and took her hand, bringing her wrist up to his nose. "Ah, my perfume. You're a very clever young man." His face reddened beneath her compliment and his smile widened shyly.

He motioned for her to get into the passenger side of the pickup, then slid in behind the wheel. All of Bonnie's uncertainty about the fitness of the truck disappeared as he started the engine with a roar. Although the exterior of the vehicle left something to be desired, the motor growled with the whine of a well-tuned, powerful race engine, and Jimmy handled the power with an expertise that belied his youth.

Bonnie held on to the cracked dashboard as they careened down the path, the ruts bouncing her up and down with breathtaking force. Tree limbs whipped and scratched the sides, making her realize why maintaining the exterior of the pickup was of little concern.

As soon as they had passed through the iron gates and were on the gravel road, Bonnie realized Jimmy could do one of two things: he could either keep his eyes on the road or he could read her lips and maintain some semblance of conversation. Bonnie opted for safety and so she settled back in the seat and stared out the window at the passing scenery.

Almost immediately her mind filled with visions of Nicholas Shepherd. Her heart quickened as she thought of his haunting words of the previous night. He'd said that evil had found a home at the Redding Institute…but what did it mean? What sort of evil? He'd walked away before she could ask any questions and she hadn't seen him this morning. His enigmatic words had kept her tossing and turning all night long and when she'd finally slept, she'd had horrid dreams…dreams filled with mutilated animals, ferocious coyotes and a creature that screamed a haunting sound of inner torment.

Brilliance bordering insanity? She dismissed what her father had said about Nicholas. She'd seen the shine of keen intelligence in his eyes, not the fervor of dementia. No, Nicholas Shepherd wasn't crazy, but he was a man with an aura of mystery, and Bonnie was definitely intrigued and drawn to him.

She sat up straighter in the seat as the gravel road turned into blacktop and farmhouses began to appear. Within minutes they were in the town, although "town" was an overly impressive term for the ten or so buildings that comprised Hollow Rock. If she hadn't heard it from Mavis, the only way she would have known the name of the place was by the big sign across the top of the post office.

Jimmy parked the truck in a space in front of the grocery store, then pulled out a list and showed Bonnie what he'd been sent to get.

She scanned the list, then looked at the nearby buildings. "Why don't we plan on meeting over there at the café in an hour," she suggested, pointing across the street where a painted rooster bid people to visit the Good Mornin' Café.

Jimmy nodded his assent and they got out of the pickup and parted ways, Jimmy heading for the grocery store and Bonnie crossing the street to the drugstore. She hoped she'd be able to pick up a couple of new paperback books.

"Can I help you with something?" The gray-haired man behind the counter eyed her with speculation as she walked through the door.

"No thanks, I'm just browsing," Bonnie replied with a polite smile as she made her way toward the magazine and book rack. The store was small, filled with the scent of stale perfume, old books and pipe tobacco.

"Don't get many browsers here in Hollow Rock," the clerk observed, his bespectacled blue eyes twinkling with friendliness. "Especially pretty ones," he added, the twinkle intensifying.

Bonnie's smile widened, recognizing the old man as a born-harmless flirter. In his day, he'd probably charmed many a woman with his sweet talk and dancing blue eyes. "I'll bet you say things like that to all your customers," she returned.

"Nope. Only the pretty ones."

Bonnie laughed and directed her attention to the magazine selection. She finally settled on her favorite fashion magazine and a mystery novel that looked intriguing.

"Nice day, ain't it," the old man said as he rang up her purchase on the antique cash register.

"Beautiful," she agreed.

"Won't be too many of these mild days left this year." He released a small moan. "Ohhh, I hate winter…the cold makes my bones hurt."

Bonnie smiled sympathetically and handed him her money.

"You visiting folks around here or just passing through?" he asked as he stuck the books in a paper sack.

"Just visiting. I'm staying out at the Redding Institute."

The bright sparkle of friendliness that had lit his eyes extinguished like a candle in the wind, leaving behind the dark hue of suspicion. "You one of them scientist types?"

"No, but my father is."

He slapped the sack down on the counter, his easy, flirtatious tone gone, swallowed up by a decidedly unfriendly aura. Without saying another word to her, he turned his back and busied himself at the back counter.

Bonnie walked out of the drugstore, confused by his reaction to her telling him where she was staying. It was obvious he didn't like someone or something at the institute. She shrugged off her unease. Whatever it was, it wasn't her problem, she thought as she checked her wristwatch. She had another half hour to kill before she met Jimmy at the café.

For the next thirty minutes, she wandered in and out of the stores, finding little of interest in any of them. Hollow Rock was obviously not a town accustomed to serving the needs of tourists.

Although everyone in the stores was relatively friendly, it was obvious the town was close-knit, unused to strangers, and not overly welcoming to people who were outsiders. She felt the curious stares of the townspeople as she walked through the small stores.

At the appropriate time, she walked into the café, looking around for Jimmy. Seeing he hadn't yet arrived, she sat down on a stool at the counter.

"What can I get you, honey?" The waitress who

approached her wore a name tag that read *Lauretta*. Her gray hair was a mass of curls that emphasized the sparkling of her eyes. Her lips curved upward in a smile that deepened the wrinkles lining her plump cheeks. Her appearance gave an impression of both eternal youth and the wisdom of years.

Bonnie returned the friendly smile. "I'd kill for a cup of coffee."

"No need for that. Just brewed a fresh pot, so you won't have to resort to no murder." The old woman's movements were deft and practiced as she reached for a cup and saucer with one hand and the coffeepot with the other. "I've got some nice hot doughnuts in back...just pulled them out of the oven."

"That sounds wonderful, but I'll wait a few minutes before I order anything else. I'm meeting someone here anytime."

Lauretta nodded, picked up a wet towel and flicked at the crumbs left by a previous customer down the counter. "Got a gorgeous morning, huh?" she said conversationally.

"Beautiful," Bonnie agreed, sipping at the hot brew.

"Only problem with days like this is the flies. This time of year, the pesky little bugs are everywhere." Lauretta replaced her wet towel with a flyswatter, slapping at a fat fly that buzzed lazily in the air. "You staying here in town or just passing through?"

Bonnie hesitated a moment before answering, remembering the reaction of the man in the drugstore. "I'm staying with family not too far from here," she finally answered. At that moment the bell above the café door tinkled, announcing a new arrival. Bonnie turned to see Jimmy come through the door. With a wave of his hand, he slid onto the stool next to her.

"Ah, one of my favorite customers." Lauretta greeted him by leaning across the counter and ruffling his carrot-colored hair. Jimmy ducked away from her hand, a shy grin stretching his mouth. "Are you with Jimmy?" Lauretta asked Bonnie curiously. Bonnie hesitated a moment, then nodded her head. "Then you must be staying out at the institute."

Again Bonnie nodded. "I was almost afraid to mention it," she confessed. "I told the clerk in the drugstore where I was staying and he instantly got extremely unfriendly."

"You'll find that most the folks around here don't much like the institute and its people. That place is Hollow Rock's version of the bogeyman."

"Why?" Bonnie asked curiously, leaning forward across the counter.

"Let me get this growing boy some doughnuts and a glass of milk," Lauretta said, pointing to Jimmy. She disappeared back into the kitchen, returning seconds later with a plate of chocolate-covered doughnuts and a glass of foaming milk. She set them down in front of Jimmy, then turned back to Bonnie.

"The folks in this neck of the woods are a backward bunch for the most part. For years there has been talk about strange goings-on at the institute, but in the last year, the talk has gotten much worse."

"Talk about what?" Bonnie pressed, remembering her own unease, her feeling of being watched, a general disquiet that had draped around her since the moment of her arrival.

"Crazy talk, mostly...about experiments and scary creatures and scientists tampering with the laws of God."

Bonnie couldn't help it—a burst of laughter bubbled to her lips. "I'm sorry," she immediately apologized. "I shouldn't laugh at other people's fears, but I've seen some of the things they're working on at the institute, and I certainly didn't see any indications of madmen tampering with the laws of God."

Lauretta nodded, her eyes retaining their twinkling friendliness. "I know, I know. Most of it is just the blathering of ignorant, small-minded people, but it all started with that deformed monkey."

"Deformed monkey?"

The old woman slowly shook her head. "The creature somehow got loose from the lab and ended up in Joe Boswell's barn. It was just a little chimpanzee, but it managed to kill two cows before Joe finally put a bullet through its brain.''

She paused a moment and poured Bonnie another cup of coffee, then continued. ''It was the damnedest thing I've ever seen...it was like the chimp was possessed by the devil himself. It wasn't right—the whole thing wasn't normal.'' Lauretta leaned forward across the counter. ''And it didn't look right.... It was deformed. It looked like a monkey, but it had the snout of a dog.''

Lauretta shivered suddenly, her voice lowered to a mere whisper. ''Old Joe, he wanted to take it to Doc Wiley—Doc is Hollow Rock's vet—but the folks from the lab came and whisked it away. Since then, relations haven't been real friendly between Hollow Rock and the institute. Of course, me, I think different. I know a couple of the men working at the institute, and I'm sure they're men of high moral fiber and good people. By the way, we never really officially introduced ourselves. I'm Lauretta Lawrence.''

''I'm Bonnie Redding.''

''Oh, I should have realized,'' Lauretta exclaimed in delight, reaching across the counter and grabbing Bonnie's hands in hers. ''I don't know why I didn't realize who you were before now. For years your father came in here two or three times a week for some of my special apple fritters. He talked a lot about his wife and daughter, even carried a picture of the two of you in his wallet.''

Warmth flooded through Bonnie at Lauretta's words. Her father did care…he'd sat here at this very counter and talked about her. He'd shown her picture to Lauretta. *He cares, he really cares,* she thought, her heart swelling.

Suddenly she couldn't wait to return to the institute, to try once again to connect with the man who apparently loved her, but who didn't seem to know how to show her.

She looked over at Jimmy, who had polished off all three of his doughnuts and now sported a milk mustache. ''Are you ready to head back?'' she asked him.

He nodded as he swiped his mouth with the back of his sleeve. Bonnie pulled her wallet from her purse and looked at Lauretta expectantly. Jimmy plucked at Bonnie's sleeve and motioned that he was going out to the truck. When he was gone, Lauretta waved her hands impatiently. ''Put your money away. Jimmy comes in here once a week for supplies. He's a good boy and I figure it's my right as owner of this dive to buy him a couple of doughnuts and a glass of milk. I reckon I can buy my friend Walter's daughter a cup of coffee, too.''

Bonnie smiled her thanks and put her wallet back in her purse. ''Wait here,'' Lauretta instructed her, disappearing once again back into the kitchen. When she emerged, she carried a small white sack which she thrust into Bonnie's hand. "Six apple fritters for Walter. That man loves my apple fritters and it's been months since he's been in for some."

"Thanks, Lauretta. I'm sure he'll be pleased." Smiling a goodbye, Bonnie left the café.

As Jimmy drove home, Bonnie leaned her head back and thought about what Lauretta had told her. A possessed, deformed monkey, a town full of wary people... She shivered as she remembered the mutilated raccoon Jimmy had found the night before. Surely that had nothing to do with lab animals and strange experiments.

When she'd been down in the lab, she hadn't seen a single sign of any animals, deformed or otherwise. Yet her mind couldn't release the memory of the strange, haunting cry she'd heard in the middle of her first night at the institute. An animal? A doomed creature of inhumane experiments?

Her mind dismissed the very idea. Her father would never be a participant in bizarre experiments. She'd seen the lab, she'd seen the computers where the scientists did the majority of their work. The stories and fears were merely the imaginations of a superstitious townspeople working overtime. Still, she couldn't wait to get back and ask her father some questions.

However, when they arrived, she realized her questions would have to wait. Mavis informed Bon-

nie that her father was in the lab and had left strict
instructions that he was not to be disturbed for any
reason. "He said he'd see you later this afternoon,"
she finished.

Bonnie swallowed her disappointment, grateful
that she'd picked up the books in the drugstore to
help pass the time. She gave Mavis the sack of apple
fritters, explaining to the older woman that Lauretta
had sent them for her father. She then started up the
stairs to her bedroom, pausing as Jimmy grabbed her
sleeve.

"What is it, Jimmy?"

Jimmy pantomimed walking, then pointed to her
and himself. "You want me to go on a walk with
you?"

He nodded his head vigorously. She considered
him for just a moment, then agreed. "Okay, just let
me put these books in my room and I'll go with
you." She took the stairs two at a time, her gaze
automatically falling on Nicholas's closed bedroom
door at the end of the hallway. She wondered if he
was in his room or downstairs in the lab. His work
hours didn't seem to be the same as those of the
other men. The others appeared to adhere to Walter's
strict schedule of hours, but Nicholas seemed to
work only when he so desired.

Bonnie frowned as she went into her bedroom and
laid the books on her bed. There was a strange sort
of inexplicable tension between her father and Nich-

olas. Professional jealousy of some sort? she wondered.

Dismissing thoughts of the brooding, handsome man and her father from her mind, she ran down the stairs to meet Jimmy.

Together, the two of them stepped out the front door and into the brilliant midmorning sunshine. "Where to?" Bonnie asked.

Jimmy smiled mysteriously, like a young child holding back a special secret. He motioned for her to follow him as he started down a tangled path that led away from the house and deeper into the surrounding forest.

At first Bonnie enjoyed the walk, noting the way the sunlight peeked through the brilliant leaves overhead and dappled the path. But as the path narrowed, and the shadows grew deeper and darker, anxiety rose inside her.

The longer they walked, the denser the brush and trees became, closing them in, surrounding them as if trying to trap them into a cage of greens and browns.

Jimmy moved with the confidence of a natural explorer, without hesitation. Bonnie hurried to keep pace with him, not wanting to lose sight of him in the tangled mass of brush and trees. There was something about this forest that made her uneasy. She didn't feel safe here.

She was about to grab Jimmy's arm and tell him

to take her back to the house when they broke into a small clearing. Directly ahead of them was the black mouth of a cave. Despite her unease, curiosity drew her toward the aperture, where nothing was visible except the shadowed darkness of perpetual night. To her surprise, Jimmy entered the darkness, motioning for her to follow him.

"Jimmy...wait!" she called after him, but he'd already turned around and so didn't see her. She hesitated only a moment before hurrying after him.

Inside, the blackness was complete, and she breathed a sigh of relief as she felt Jimmy's hand reach for hers. She gripped his painfully tight, communicating her unease to him. He returned her squeeze as they walked deeper into the darkness. The passageway they were in narrowed, the walls moving closer and closer. She could hear the trickle of water somewhere in the distance. After a moment or two, Bonnie noticed the dark was less deep, that ahead was the glow of daylight.

She expelled a sigh of relief as they stepped out of the narrow passageway and into a huge room where sunlight peeked through holes in the high ceiling and danced on the stream that gurgled over a rocky bed. "Oh, Jimmy," she exclaimed, awed by the beauty nature had created in the underground cavern. She released his hand and walked over to the edge of the stream. Strangely shaped limestone deposits hung down from the high ceiling like icicles and rose up from the floor like otherworldly creatures.

"Beautiful, isn't it?"

Bonnie gasped and whirled around at the sound of the deep voice that echoed for a lingering moment. He stood in the shadows against one of the walls. "Must you always sneak up on me?" she snapped, her gaze darting around the cavern.

"If you're looking for Jimmy, he's gone," Nicholas said, moving toward her with his animal-like grace. "I asked him to bring you here." He moved closer to her, so close she could smell his provocative scent. She wondered if it emanated from some cologne he put on, or if it radiated naturally from his skin.

She felt her heartbeat ticking anxiously at her temples as the heat from his body reached out warm fingers and embraced her. She took a step back from him. "What...what do you want?"

"I wanted to talk to you away from the institute, where the walls have ears." With a graceful agility, he sat down by the edge of the stream, motioning for her to join him.

She hesitated a moment, unsure what was more dangerous, running out of the cave and into the unknown forest, or sitting down beside Nicholas Shepherd. She laughed inwardly at her own silliness. There was nothing dangerous about Nicholas. He was a man of science and knowledge.

Still, as she eased herself down next to him, she realized there was a sense of wildness about him that called on something deep within herself, an element she hadn't known she possessed until this very moment. "What did you want to talk to me about?" she asked, carefully keeping enough distance between them that there wouldn't be an inadvertent touch, a brush of thighs or shoulders.

For a moment he stared into the stream, his features taut with concentration. She took the opportunity to study him, noting the strength and beauty of his facial features. She was surprised to realize that his eyes weren't silver as she'd originally thought. They were the green of a primeval forest, holding the mysteries of such a place. However, when he turned to look at her, the sunlight reflected off the water and his eyes once again retained a strange, silvery glow that banished the natural green hue. "You must leave the institute immediately."

"Why?" she asked, startled by his vehemence, the controlled emotion his voice radiated.

"You are in danger here. Go back to your life and forget about your father."

"I can't do that.... I won't do that," Bonnie answered firmly. "I've waited too long to have this opportunity with my father."

Again, his gaze sought the stream and he took several deep breaths, as if trying to steady the emotions that tensed his body, radiated from him in thick waves of energy. "Things aren't what they seem to be at the institute. Your fath—Walter is a man driven by obsession, possessed with a need that leaves no room for compassion or mercy." He turned and looked at her once again, the intensity in his gaze stealing her breath away. "He will use any means available, anyone he must to achieve his ungodly goals."

"I don't believe you." The words escaped Bonnie in a whisper. "You talk like my father is evil, and I know he isn't...he couldn't be."

With a swiftness of movement, Nicholas grabbed her by the shoulders. "How would you know?" he demanded. "How would you know what he's like? You know nothing about him...nothing."

"I know the man my mother fell in love with. The man she married isn't capable of the things you say."

He stared at her for a long moment, the intensity in his eyes fading as his hands eased their strength on her shoulders. He didn't remove his grip on her shoulders, but his hands now caressed, each movement filling Bonnie with a strange kind of heat.

"What?" she asked, feeling that he wanted to say more, needed to say more, but he merely shook his head, frustration twisting his features into a semblance of hopelessness.

He drew a deep breath and closed his eyes for a moment, and when he opened them again they had returned to the forest-green color. "Bonnie, you've lived this long without having a relationship with your father. Keep the few good memories you have of him safe in your heart.... Leave the Redding Institute now...today."

Bonnie searched his face, more confused than she'd ever been in her life. Her father had warned her about Nicholas's insanity, but it wasn't madness she saw in his eyes. She saw genuine concern, and beneath that the flicker of an emotion that drew her to him. His hands on her shoulders burned into her blouse with their heat, speaking to her in words quite different than what he said. "I can't leave," she finally said. "Not yet. I don't care about whatever experiments are going on here. I've waited a long time to get to know my father, and I'm not going to waste this chance. And I don't believe he's capable of the things you say he is."

"Why? Because you think parenthood is synonymous with sainthood? Don't you believe that parents are as susceptible to greed as anyone?"

There was a bitterness in his tone, a bitterness that Bonnie instinctively knew had nothing to do with her situation, but rather one that stemmed from his own childhood. "What about your parents, Nicholas? Where are they?"

He released his hold on her and ran a hand through his thick, dark hair. "Who knows? I haven't seen them since I was eight years old."

"Why?"

A ragged sigh escaped his lips, one that tugged at Bonnie's heart. He picked up a small stone and tossed it into the stream, focused on the ripple effect that resulted. "From the time I was three years old, it was obvious that I was different. I could take apart and put together any machine or electrical device I was given. The testing began when I started school and it was discovered I was doing college-level work. My parents were poor and uneducated. To them I was a freak, a changeling. I think I frightened them more than just a little bit."

He picked up another rock and studied it a moment before tossing it into the water. "Anyway, it wasn't until somebody came to talk to them about putting me in a special school that they suddenly realized I might be a valuable commodity." He looked at her, his eyes once again sparking with a dangerous silver light. "They put a price on my head and sold me."

"Sold you?" She looked at him incredulously.

"What else do you call it when they get paid to give me to a think tank? I went to school and I never saw them again."

Bonnie ached with the hurt she knew was inside him, a hurt not unlike the one she'd harbored all these years. They were both wounded children on the inside, yearning for something it was probably too late to ever attain…the unconditional love of parents.

Was this bitterness and hurt inside him what had prompted his words about her own father? Had his own pain skewed his vision of fathers and mothers everywhere? It suddenly didn't matter what he'd said about her father—what mattered was her need to comfort him.

She reached out and placed a hand on his arm, feeling the sinewy muscle beneath the cotton shirt. "I'm so sorry, Nicholas," she said softly.

The silver glint of his eyes increased. "Don't waste your pity on me. I may be one of the damned, but the last thing I want from you is pity."

Pity? No, that wasn't what Bonnie felt at the moment. As she stared into his strange eyes, with his scent enveloping her, she felt a very different emotion. It made her heart quicken and her mouth grow dry. And she recognized it as desire when his lips began to descend toward hers.

Thought swirled out of her head as his mouth captured hers. Instinctively she opened to him, inviting his tongue to delve inside. His lips were hot, melting away any rational reason why she shouldn't kiss him. There was a wildness in him as his arms wrapped around her. He tasted of cold winds blowing through a dark forest and deep mysteries unexplored. He tasted of a primitive man without the veneer of civilized thought.

Bonnie's response to him was immediate, a hot wind of desire that blew through her veins, heating and thickening her blood as it pulsed inside her. The kiss wrapped around her, enfolding her in a heat that was all-consuming, and she wanted it to go on forever.

She wasn't sure when it changed, when she felt a new, frightening tension radiating from his body. Raw energy, in its most base form, emanated from him, and with a harsh moan he shoved her away. In one swift movement he stood up and turned his back on her. "Get out of here, Bonnie."

She stood up, confusion mingling with the other emotions he'd stroked from her. She saw the taut pull of all his muscles, realized that he was fighting some internal battle. "Nicholas?" She mentally willed him to turn around, tell her what was happening, but his back remained rigidly toward her.

"Get out of here. Get away from me." His voice thundered in the cavern, echoing ominously throughout. Something tugged on her sleeve and she turned to see Jimmy, his face blanched of color, his eyes transmitting urgency. He grabbed her hand and pulled her after him, into the dark passageway, then out of the cave itself.

"Jimmy...wait. What's happening? What about Nicholas?" She tried to release his grip on her hand, but he shook his head vehemently and pulled her after him in a race through the woods.

As they ran, Bonnie's mind whirled with questions. What was happening? Why were they running as if the very devil himself was nipping at their heels? If there was danger, then why hadn't Nicholas run away with them?

They had nearly reached the house when Bonnie finally managed to jerk her hand out of Jimmy's. She leaned against a tree trunk and fought to catch her breath. She panted from the exertion, a breath clogging her throat as she heard the distant cry of some animal. A deep bellow of rage, a mournful cry of injustice, a primitive inhuman sound, it rang through the trees and sent goose bumps racing up her spine. It came from the direction of the cave, and she didn't know whether to be afraid *for* Nicholas, or *of* him.

Nicholas ran through the woods, away from the institute and deeper into the forest. There wasn't enough time to make it back to the safety of the special room. The change would be upon him too quickly. Already his skin burned and prickled, portending what was to come. It was too late to alter the inevitable. The only thing he could hope for was that he would get far enough into the forest, far enough away so he couldn't harm anyone... especially her.

Bonnie... Her name echoed over and over again in the dark corners of his wavering consciousness. Soon the image of her in his mind would be swallowed up by the darkness that always came with the change.

If only he hadn't kissed her. If only he hadn't tasted the sweet innocence of her lips. It had not merely stirred the embers of desire, it had also reminded him that he wasn't normal, might never be normal again. And it had been that thought that had agitated the anger that was never very far from the surface.

He stopped running, sinking to the ground as pinpoints of pain ripped through him. A searing white heat unfurled in his stomach and an excruciating pounding boomed in his head. His last conscious thought was that he would somehow force Bonnie to leave the institute immediately. He had a feeling that soon he would have no control at all over his transformations. The rage—his anger—would completely consume him, and when that happened nobody would ever be safe around him again.

CHAPTER FIVE

"Where's Nicholas?" Bonnie asked as they all sat down to dinner that evening. She'd spent most of the afternoon up in her room, trying to figure out what had happened in the cave. After she'd heard the strange animal cry, she'd questioned Jimmy but had learned nothing...only that the animal was a coyote or a wolf and that Nicholas could take care of himself.

"Nicholas is working down in the lab. He won't be joining us for dinner," Walter explained, cutting into his pork roast with the gusto he seemed to bring to every meal.

As the men talked, Bonnie watched her father, trying to discern some of the qualities Nicholas had warned her about. It was true, his face held more animation when the conversation revolved around his work, but surely that didn't make him a bad man. She couldn't take Nicholas's warnings seriously. His view of fathers was tainted by his own father's apparent betrayal.

"You know, my dear, I've been meaning to speak to you about Nicholas," Walter said, pulling Bonnie guiltily from her thoughts.

"What about him?" she asked guardedly, wondering if it was possible her father was privy to what had gone on in the cave between them.

"I'm afraid I was a bit too harsh on him when you first arrived." He smiled charmingly. "I was angry at him and said things about him that I didn't mean. Actually, I hope you will get to know Nicholas, spend some time with him. I think he could use a companion." As he smiled at her, she knew there was no way her father was the evil monster Nicholas had tried to make her believe.

He might be obsessed, he might get caught up in his own little world of experiments and analysis, but at heart he was a good man, and his observations about Nicholas only proved the fact.

She thoughtfully chewed a bite of the succulent pork. And Nicholas? She wasn't sure what she thought of him. Certainly his kiss had taken her by surprise, stirring in her a desire to know him better, to learn about the mysteries that darkened his eyes.

"Oh, by the way, did you get the sack that Lauretta sent for you?" she asked her father, suddenly remembering the doughnuts the woman had sent back with her. "She said her apple fritters were favorites of yours."

"Yes, I ate them this afternoon," Walter replied.

"She seems friendly," Bonnie continued. "She certainly spoke highly of you." Walter merely grunted and returned his attention to the food on his plate. "In fact, she told me about a crazed, deformed laboratory monkey that wreaked havoc in Hollow Rock. I don't remember seeing any animals down in the lab.''

Walter slammed his fork down on the table, bits of meat spewing across the pristine lace cloth. ''That woman and her blathering mouth,'' he exploded. He instantly took a deep breath and smiled an apology to Bonnie. ''I'm sorry, it just makes me so angry to hear that she's speaking such nonsense. That's half the reason why the people of Hollow Rock think we're part of the devil's plot to ruin the world.'' He paused a moment to take a drink of water, then continued. ''Yes, at one time we were using animals here, a distasteful, but necessary part of science. The monkey that got loose was neither crazed nor deformed. It suffered from an inoperable brain tumor that made its behavior violent and erratic. After that, I decided to do away with the animal experiments. Unfortunately, it isn't so easy to dispel the ignorant gossip of uneducated, superstitious people.''

''So if you don't use animals anymore, how do you test whatever it is you're working on?'' Bonnie asked curiously.

''Ah, the marvels of today's computers. We can simulate unbelievable things just by pushing a couple of keys.'' Once again Walter's face lit up with pleasure as he launched into a monologue on the improvements of modern technology. The other men joined in and Bonnie feigned interest, but her mind wandered, unable to follow their scientific jargon.

She wasn't surprised when immediately after dinner her father and the three other men disappeared back into the lab. She was rapidly getting accustomed to spending long periods of time by herself. She tapped down her growing sense of frustration as she went into the living room and sat down.

Why had her father finally agreed to let her come to visit him if he didn't intend to take the time to visit with her?

With a deep sigh, she decided to go up to her room and take a long, hot bath. A few minutes later, as she relaxed in the water in the tub, she thought again about those moments spent with Nicholas in the cave. There had been several times when she'd thought he wanted to tell her something—something important—but for some reason he'd held back.

She shivered suddenly despite the warmth of the water as she remembered those moments when she'd tasted his delicious mouth, felt the strength of his muscles beneath her fingertips. It had been like being in an embrace with a wild animal.

She leaned her head back and closed her eyes, allowing the heat that surrounded her to lull her into a state of complete relaxation. Yes, an animal…that's exactly what Nicholas reminded her of with his strange, glowing eyes and taut, lean physique.

She wasn't sure how much time passed. It might

have been seconds, it could have been hours, when she heard the bathroom door creak on its rusty hinges. She turned her head and there he was.

He stood there, filling the doorway, his eyes glowing like slivers of the moon. He was naked except for the thick carpet of dark hair that covered his chest, and her breath caught in her throat as she saw the power of his physique, the beauty of symmetry.

She didn't realize she was in her bed until he joined her there, warming her body with the heat from his as he wrapped his arms around her. Although his eyes radiated the wild hunger of a beast, his touch was soft and gentle as he caressed the length of her naked flesh. His hands were smooth, tender, as he captured the fullness of her breasts.

She didn't think to protest. She knew she'd been lost the moment he'd come through the bathroom door and she'd fallen into the glow of his eyes. And, in any case, she didn't want to protest...she wanted him and all he had to give to her.

As his fingertips traced little circles around her turgid nipples, his mouth found hers in a hungry kiss that made her shiver to her very soul. His mouth was hot and demanding and she took his demand and returned it with her own, arching against him with a base need.

His hands moved down the smooth flatness of her stomach, across her sleek thighs, and as he raised up to look deeply into her eyes once again, she knew he was a man who loved the touch, the scent, the taste of a woman.

As he dipped his head to taste one of her aching nipples, she closed her eyes, moaning and tangling her hands in his thick head of hair.

His mouth was magic, coaxing and teasing, nipping and kissing. Exquisite sensations rippled through her, turning her insides to molten liquid. There was no part of her body he didn't explore with gentle fingers and his caressing mouth. He found each and every zone of pleasure and spent endless moments stroking her, loving her.

Her window was open, a cool night breeze flapping the curtains and stimulating further their heated flesh. As his mouth moved from her breast to lick and nip at her stomach, she gasped in pure pleasure, wondering if it was possible to die from too much arousal.

Her eyes flickered open and she caught sight of the full moon that hung just outside the window, its silvery light cascading down like shining tinsel. It startled her. How had it gotten so full so fast?

There was a sense of unreality about everything. The moonlight cast dancing shadows on the wall. The cool breeze blew in whispers of the night. The scent of Nicholas and the crisp air outside mingled to create a smell that only fed her desire.

Nicholas said not a word, but his hands and mouth communicated eloquently as they explored every part of her body. As he worked his magic, she felt the crest of a huge wave approaching, and she surrendered entirely to him. The wave swept over her, through her, and she cried out his name as again and again she rode the tide of pleasure.

And then he was on her, in her, filling her with his heat. She welcomed him, her hands splaying against his muscular back, moving to memorize the sinewy patterns beneath his skin. As she buried her head against the soft heat of his neck, she thought she heard a deep growl, but the strange noise was quickly swallowed by her own sounds of passion and want.

At first he moved with a slow deliberation, as if his primary desire was to give her the most intense pleasure she'd ever experienced. And he did. Her body blossomed beneath his, eagerly accepting all he had to give, urging him deeper, harder. As his pace increased, she felt a new tension hardening his muscles, a raw energy pulsating off him. She felt his imminent release and encouraged it, wanting to share the ultimate high with him.

She turned her head to the side, moaning deep in her throat, and her gaze caught their shapes silhouetted against the wall. Someplace in the back of her passion-fogged mind, she recognized the silhouette of herself lying prone…but something was wrong with his silhouette…it was the shadow of a beast…a… wolf.

She jerked her gaze back to look at him, and she saw only Nicholas, his eyes brilliant with desire. She looked back at the wall, back at him…back at the wall….A wolf—yes, that was what he reminded her of…big, black timber wolf.

Suddenly his back beneath her hands was soft with fur and his body seemed to expand beneath her fingertips. The room exploded, filling with a terrifying howl. She was afraid to look at him again, afraid of what she might see. She squeezed her eyes tightly closed and opened her mouth to scream.

She choked, spitting out water as she sat straight up in the bathtub. She looked around wildly, for a moment disoriented, wondering how she had gotten from the bed back to the tub. Where was he? Where had he gone?

She stared at the bathroom door, realizing it was still locked. Nobody had come in.

A dream…it had all been a crazy dream. She expelled a shuddery sigh and rubbed the back of her neck where a kink had appeared. A dream…a nightmare. She shivered, realizing the water surrounding her was no longer warm and inviting, but cold as a grave. My God, where had such images come from? What had provoked such a bizarre, achingly vivid nightmare?

Arising, she grabbed a towel, her body still tingling with the remembered sensations from the dream. She felt ill, as if consumed by a high fever, but she knew it was merely the lingering effects of the erotic images that had filled her nightmare.

She dried off, then stared at her reflection in the mirror, wondering what on earth had possessed her to entertain such a dream. She looked normal enough, so what possible anomaly could her mind contain that would stimulate a dream about a...werewolf?

A slow grin gradually lifted the corners of her mouth. A werewolf, indeed. And she also believed in vampires, Frankenstein and people-eating worms. She shook her head ruefully. She was letting this place and the people get to her.

It must have been the combination of Nicholas's kiss in the cave and the scream of the wild animal that had formed the strange vision.

She reached up and touched her lips, remembering the searing heat that had marked them when his mouth had kissed hers. She wasn't sure what frightened her more—the lingering effects of her nightmarish visions of Nicholas as a wolf, or the remaining effect of his lips tasting hers. Of course, the difference was that Nicholas had really kissed her, and he certainly was no werewolf.

Leaving the bathroom, she went into the bedroom, where the light of dusk was whispering goodbye and being swallowed up by the black of night. She pulled her nightgown on and looked at the clock, surprised to realize she'd lost nearly an hour in the tub.

"Terrific," she muttered dryly. After a nap like that, she'd be awake half the night.

She threw herself across the bed and picked up the

magazine she'd bought earlier in the day. Maybe the pages of fashion and glamour tips would take her mind off the fact that she was no closer to her father than she'd been before arriving, and dangerously closer to a man she didn't quite trust.

It was nearly midnight when she looked at the clock and closed the magazine, sleep still as elusive as ever. She walked over to the window and looked out, the moon not full, but rather a nearly perfect three-quarter slice of distant light. The dim light spilling down cast an eerie illumination on the trees below. Their autumn leaves danced and shuddered in the night breeze, making them look like strange silhouettes of alien creatures. Again she felt as if there was something dark and sinister about the forest, as though it housed an evil unspeakable.

She forced another smile. She was definitely letting this place get to her. This was a laboratory of science, not one of evil. This was her father's house, so to speak, and her father would never allow evil to dwell here.

She turned away from the window and grabbed her robe. Maybe she'd sneak downstairs to the kitchen and fix herself a glass of milk. Maybe that would help her get to sleep.

The darkness in the hallway was complete as she made her way down the stairs like a blind person. Once she reached the bottom of the stairs, the moonlight peeking into the windows led her way through the dining room and toward the swinging kitchen doors. She paused for a moment, not relishing the idea of meeting the unfriendly Mavis in the middle of the night. She had a feeling the woman would be as territorial as a pit bull concerning the kitchen.

With a deep breath, she pushed through the doors, relieved to find the area completely deserted. She flipped on the light above the stove, then searched the cabinets until she found the one containing the glasses.

She poured herself a large glass of milk and sat down on one of the wooden stools at the work counter. As she sipped the cold milk, she looked around curiously, surprised to see that the kitchen was completely updated and held every cooking convenience ever invented. No wonder Mavis was able to prepare culinary delights here, she mused.

Her heart clenched as she thought of her mother's tiny kitchen, with the stove that was nearly as old as Bonnie herself. Two burners hadn't worked properly, either undercooking or overcooking everything. Her mother would have loved this kitchen, with its large size and modern equipment. Again Bonnie was struck with a small ball of resentment hitting her right in the chest. It didn't seem fair that her father had lived here all these years and her mother had existed in a small three-bedroom home.

Bonnie had tried and tried to convince her mother to move into an apartment, one of those places with new carpeting and airy windows, but her mother had been adamant that she needed to stay in the house she and her husband had bought together. "When he finally comes home, how will he know where to find us if we move?" she'd said whenever Bonnie broached the subject.

She jumped as the kitchen doors suddenly swung open and Nicholas entered. He stopped abruptly at the sight of her, his facial features tightening. "Oh, I didn't know anyone else was still up." He moved into the room and to the refrigerator.

"I couldn't sleep," Bonnie replied, watching him as he poured himself a large glass of milk and cut off a piece of the cherry pie they'd had for dessert earlier in the evening.

She pulled the belt of her robe tighter, the memory of their shared kiss and her strangely erotic, disturbing dream too fresh in her mind for her to feel completely comfortable with him.

He joined her at the counter, bringing with him the scent that belonged to him alone, an evocative scent that stirred her deep inside. "I was hoping you'd have packed up your bags and left this place."

"I don't intend to leave," Bonnie returned, a deep frustration welling up within her. "Getting to know my father is something I need to do. I spent too many years wondering about him, fantasizing about him, to just pack my bags and leave." She paused a moment and took a deep breath, then continued. "My mother spoke about my father as if he were a saint. You speak of him as if he's the devil himself. I have to make up my own mind about what he is and what he isn't."

Nicholas released a sigh of weary resignation. He splayed his hand and ran it through his hair, and Bonnie noticed the lines of tiredness that had deepened around his eyes. "You're as big a fool as I was," he answered.

"What do you mean?"

He gazed at her, and she got a feeling that his strange, glowing eyes were trying to communicate something, some unknown danger, to her, but he merely shook his head. "It doesn't matter," he finally said, focusing his attention on his pie.

She watched him for a moment. Although his face was all hard lines and angles, holding a sternness that daunted, there was something about it that also compelled. At this moment, the hardness was tempered with the look of profound weariness, and Bonnie fought the impulse to reach out and stroke the side of his cheek, relieve the tension that existed there. "Why aren't you in bed?" she asked.

"I've been working down in the lab."

"Pretty long hours," she observed.

"It's a pretty important project," he returned.

"Why do you work such different hours from the rest of the men?"

"I'm not working on the same things as they are."

When he didn't offer more, Bonnie pressed him, wanting to know everything about him, what made him tick, what he loved and what he hated. "So, what are you working on?"

Again his gaze sought hers, and she sensed he wanted to talk, wanted to tell her something, share knowledge that weighed heavily on his soul, but his eyes glazed over and his facial muscles tightened. "It's the most important project I'll ever work on…and it's completely personal." There was a finality to his tone that forbade her asking anything else.

As he once again concentrated on eating his pie, she studied him again, wondering what it was about him that so fascinated her, drew her toward him like two atoms destined to collide and merge together. There was something about him that frightened her, but it was a fascinating fear in its mysterious source.

"I was worried about you this afternoon when we left you in the cave," she said.

His eyes flickered in surprise, as if it had never occurred to him that anyone would ever be concerned for him. "There was no reason to worry."

"But we heard an animal…. It sounded like a coyote or a wolf."

He smiled, a slow, enigmatic one that caused her heart to thud dangerously fast in her chest. "Even the most ferocious beasts give me a wide berth." He pushed away from the counter and carried his dishes to the sink. When he turned to face her once again, his eyes were silver orbs. "You might do well to remember that." With this, he strode out of the room.

Bonnie expelled a breath when he was gone, willing her heartbeat to slow down its rapid pace. Warnings...that's all she seemed to be hearing lately.... Vague warnings from her father about Nicholas, from Nicholas about her father...from Nicholas about himself. She felt as if she'd been plunged into an alien world where everyone was speaking a language she only half understood. With a sigh, she carried her glass over to the sink and added it to Nicholas's dirty dishes. Then, thinking of Mavis's reaction when she saw the dishes in the morning, Bonnie quickly washed them and placed them in the drainer.

She performed the duty by rote, her mind still whirling with remnant pieces of the day. Lauretta's words, Nicholas's warnings, her father's continued distance... Like pieces of a patchwork quilt, she knew they all had a place, but they wouldn't make any sense until they were carefully sewn together.

But no matter how hard she tried, they remained unconnected, disjointed, nonsensical to the point of impotent frustration. "Damn," she muttered, setting the last dish in the drainer. She folded the dish towel and got ready to leave the kitchen, her footsteps halted by something white that caught her attention in the trash can by the stove.

She frowned and approached the black plastic can.

On top of the other garbage was the white sack she'd brought back from town...the one Lauretta had given her filled with apple fritters.

Curiosity killed the cat. The old proverb taunted her. But curiosity also provides answers, she countered. She picked up the bag and reached inside. Slowly, she pulled out the apple fritters...all six of them. They had not been eaten that afternoon as her father had told her. They were all here in front of her. Why had he told her he'd eaten them? Why had he lied? If they were a favorite of his, why had they been thrown away? None of this made any sense whatsoever.

She put them back in the bag, then placed the bag back in the can and shut off the light above the stove. *No, curiosity doesn't always provide answers,* she thought. *Sometimes it simply makes more questions.*

CHAPTER SIX

Bonnie sat in the library, drumming her fingers on the wooden table at her side, wondering if it was possible to die from boredom.

She'd now been here over a week. She'd spent almost no time with her father except for meals, when they were surrounded by his cohorts.

Boredom was the wrong word, she thought, rising out of the chair and pacing the room restlessly. Frustrated…that was what she was. She'd come here with a specific goal in mind—to discover the essence of the man who had fathered her—but she was no closer to attaining her goal than she'd been back home with no contact with him whatsoever.

In fact, she was beginning to feel as if she suffered from some dread social disease. Other than the brief conversation with Nicholas in the kitchen three nights before, she'd hardly seen him, either. She wondered if everyone was intentionally avoiding her.

Tonight she was going to pin down her father, force him to sit down and talk to her about the past, about decisions he'd made that had concerned her and her mother. In the meantime, she'd find Jimmy and see what he was doing. At least his bright smile told her he was always glad to see her.

Jimmy proved as elusive as a red-winged butterfly. She looked for him all over the house. Not finding him, she continued her search outside on the grounds.

She was nearly ready to give up and go back to her room when she heard a burst of deep laughter coming from the edge of the copse of trees. She knew immediately it was Nicholas's laughter, and the alien sound of it warmed her insides.

She moved closer, the sound drawing her toward it like the Pied Piper's magical tune. She crept softly, not wanting him to see her. She somehow knew that if he saw her the laughter would stop, and she wanted to see him laughing, needed to see his facial muscles relaxed and free of tension.

As she drew closer and peered through the thick foliage, she saw them—Jimmy and Nicholas sitting on the trunk of a dead, fallen tree in the middle of a small clearing. The sunlight overhead sneaked in through the leaves, dancing in delight on Jimmy's copper hair. Nicholas's dark hair seemed to absorb the light, as not a single highlight shone from its dark richness.

But it was Nicholas's face that captured her attention. She'd always recognized he was handsome, with a face of almost brutal strength. Now, as she saw the smile that curved his lips and brightened his eyes, she realized it was a nice face, a face that held a hint of compassion and gentleness.

"Okay, Jimmy. Let's try it again," Nicholas instructed, holding his hands out in front of him. Jimmy nodded and did the same. *"A...B...C..."*

As Bonnie watched, they ran through the alphabet, their fingers manipulating the letters in sign language. Several times Jimmy faltered, frowning with frustration, but Nicholas encouraged and cajoled, exhibiting infinite patience. When Jimmy made the wrong sign, Nicholas laughed and ruffled the young man's hair in obvious affection.

It was a poignant scene, one that tore at Bonnie's heart. Perhaps her father was right. Perhaps Nicholas really did need a friend, something besides the companionship of a deaf boy. She was struck by the fact that she, Nicholas and Jimmy all shared the pain of being fatherless. Maybe they could all help each other in healing the pains of childhood. At least, it was a nice thought.

Without waiting for hesitation to set in, she parted the tree limbs and stepped through, smiling in greeting. "I thought I heard somebody in here," she said, noting in dismay how Nicholas's features instantly tightened, tension usurping his easy relaxation of moments before.

"Jimmy, that will be all for today," Nicholas said. Jimmy nodded, and with a wave to Bonnie, he stood up and walked off in the direction of the house.

"You didn't have to stop on my account," Bonnie protested.

Nicholas shrugged. "We'd been working for about an hour, anyway. It was time to quit."

Bonnie stepped over and sat down in the space Jimmy had vacated on the log next to Nicholas. "It's wonderful that you're taking the time to teach Jimmy how to sign. It will open up a whole new world of communication to him."

Nicholas frowned. "He should be attending a special school. He should have been taught how to sign years ago."

"Why wasn't he?"

"Who knows? Mavis doesn't know sign language, and I guess nobody else ever took the time with him. He's such a bright kid…it's a sin that he hasn't had any formal education at all."

Bonnie looked at him in surprise. "What do you mean? Surely he's attended school?"

He shook his head, the sun once again finding his dark head and giving his hair a lustrous sheen. "The Hollow Rock school system is hardly equipped to handle any kid with special needs. From what Mavis told me, he went to school for a couple of days when he was younger, then never went back. The kids teased him and the teachers didn't know what to do with him."

"But what about the law that demands kids go to school for a certain number of years?" Bonnie asked incredulously.

Nicholas looked at her wryly. "A law is only a law

if somebody enforces it. Nobody cared enough about Jimmy. Besides, after those first couple of days, Jimmy didn't want to go back and face the other students. Teasing and taunts hurt no less when you're deaf.''

"That's so sad," Bonnie said with a heavy sigh, tilting her head back to study the colorful leaf canopy overhead. "Kids can be so cruel to each other.''

Nicholas snorted in disbelief. "What would you know about that?''

She looked at him, noting how the shadows caressed his face, lingering in the hollows, emphasizing the angles. She wished he would laugh again. She wanted his face to light up from within, erasing the lines of rigid control, the clench of his jaw. Why was he so tense whenever she was around? "It doesn't matter," she finally said, not wanting to dredge up old childhood traumas.

"But it does," he countered, searching her face with perplexity. "I can't imagine why any kids would be cruel to you.''

She smiled and stretched her legs out in front of her, finding a more comfortable position as her mind whirled her back in time. "When I was growing up, single-parent families were less the norm than they are now. I only had one friend whose parents were divorced." Her smile slowly faded as memories flooded back. "I went through a period when it was incredibly important to me that all my friends understand my parents weren't divorced...that my father hadn't left us and just walked away for another woman or because he was unhappy. But all they saw was that he wasn't there, he didn't live with us. They couldn't understand it, and how could I explain it to them? I didn't understand it myself.''

She frowned, staring down at her worn tennis shoes. ''They teased me, told me he didn't care about us at all, and I was just lying about him being an important scientist. Eventually, I quit talking about him. I even pretended he was dead.'' She looked back at Nicholas. ''Someplace deep inside me, it's important that I vindicate myself and my father. I'm not sure what is more important, somehow proving that he loved me to myself, or to all the other taunting voices that occasionally sound off in my head.''

''Perhaps you should have just kept on pretending he was dead,'' Nicholas said harshly.

''That's a horrible thing to say,'' Bonnie retorted swiftly. ''On the heels of my mother's death, I don't think I could handle it if something happened to my dad.''

Nicholas's face tightened, and once again Bonnie got the feeling there was something he wanted to tell her, something he needed to say, but he compressed his lips together, his eyes radiating secrets he wouldn't—or couldn't—share.

''What about you, Nicholas? Did you have friends at the school you attended when you were younger?''

The tension ebbed from his features and he smiled dryly. "A think tank for a bunch of kids doesn't exactly encourage friendships. We were taught to compete and discouraged from forming any real attachments to any one person."

"Sounds like a horrid place," she replied softly. *Perhaps this explains his separateness from the others,* she thought. Socialization, friendships…these were all skills that were taught, and apparently even people with genius IQs needed lessons in such things.

It was her sense of his incredible aloneness that drew her to him, that combined with a mysterious force that whispered of dangerous, turbulent waters and overwhelming, secretive depths. She looked at him again, trying to discern the essence of him, needing to understand what caused the strange energy that emanated from him, the haunting mist that veiled his unusual eyes.

"So, how did you get from the school to this place in the backwoods of Arkansas?" Bonnie asked curiously.

"I was working for a government agency when I was approached by Jonathon and Walter, recruited to come to this place and work for them. That was almost a year ago." Nicholas stood up suddenly and began to pace back and forth in front of her. Again she felt the radiation of strange energy in the air, like electricity crackling around him, through him. "They promised me unlimited funds, whatever equipment I wanted, hours I chose myself.... It would have sounded like paradise to any scientist.'' He stopped pacing and looked at her, his eyes flickering first their deep green, then a silver hue. A trick of the sunlight, she thought, suddenly frightened as the power around him seemed to intensify. ''And the only price I paid for this scientist's utopia was my soul.'' His eyes flickered even more metallic. ''I've got to go,'' he said, and he turned and walked into the deep brush nearby, disappearing instantly.

Bonnie stared after him, filled with an incredible frustration that bordered on anger. Damn him. It wasn't fair for him to casually drop these enigmatic, strange statements, then walk away. She reached out and picked a dead leaf off the nearby tree limb. Crumpling it in her fist, she watched the pieces drift to the ground at her feet. Pieces...that's all she had of the puzzle, and the longer she remained here the more pieces there were and the more difficult it was to discount their importance.

Something was amiss here...something wasn't right. She was becoming more and more intrigued with the mysteries hiding in the shadows at the Redding Institute.

She sighed and brushed her hands together, removing the residue of crushed leaves. She frowned, thinking of Nicholas's words. *He'd paid with his soul for the opportunity to work here.* What did that mean? How had he paid with his soul?

With another sigh of frustration, she stood up and brushed off the seat of her jeans. She turned to start back to the house, but froze as she heard the sound of a branch snapping. The sound exploded in the quiet of the woods. A wild, animal scent assailed her nose, not unpleasant, but alien to her senses. Slowly, she turned and looked around, the hairs on the back of her neck prickling as she heard the rumble of a low growl.

Her gaze searched the surrounding woods, her eyes widening in terror as she saw the wolf, staring at her from his hiding place amid the tangled underbrush.

She knew she should run—the warning of imminent danger pumped wildly through her veins—but she remained frozen, unable to move in her intense fear.

For an infinite moment they remained facing each other, the wolf's eyes predatory, reflecting a wild hunger that Bonnie knew nothing could ever satisfy. He was a huge animal, far bigger than Bonnie had ever thought a wolf to be, and his fur was a dark gray blending into shadowed darkness across his head and forelegs.

As Bonnie watched, the wolf picked up a front paw and stealthily took a step toward her. Bonnie took a single step back. As if in a macabre dance, the wolf moved forward and again Bonnie stepped back. At the same time, his powerful jaws opened, showing glittering, sharp teeth. He growled…a deep, thunderous, savage sound that instantly snapped Bonnie's mental paralysis.

Crying out in terror, she whirled around and ran for the house. She heard the branches snap and pop behind her, but she didn't turn around. She was afraid to look back.

She ran as she never had before, with each step expecting to feel the searing pain of claws ripping down her back, ferocious teeth gnashing at her flesh. She gasped in painful grunts, her gaze focused intently on the front door and the safety that lay behind it.

She hit the door with a thud, yanking it open and falling inside.

"My dear, whatever is wrong?"

A sob caught in her throat as she saw her father through a mist of tears. Without conscious thought she threw herself into his arms, needing the strength, the protection of her father to soothe her fear.

She clung to him like a young child, disappointed when his arms didn't gently enfold her, but rather grabbed her by the shoulders and held her away from him. "For God's sake, Bonnie, get hold of yourself and tell me what's wrong," he demanded.

Bonnie stepped away from him, instantly embarrassed by her display of emotions. "I'm sorry," she apologized, gulping back one last sob. She swiped at her tears and took a deep breath to steady herself. "There was a wolf in the woods...a big gray wolf."

She wrapped her arms tightly around herself to ward off a deep shudder.

"Did he have black markings?" Walter asked, his attention riveted on her. "Around his face and neck?"

"Y-yes. How did you know?"

"How did he react when he saw you?"

Bonnie frowned, finding her father's questions puzzling. She shrugged her shoulders helplessly. "I don't know. I guess he reacted like any wolf. He growled at me and...I think he chased me, but I'm not sure. I didn't stop to look back to see what he was doing."

Walter grunted, his concentration obviously focused inward rather than on her. He smiled suddenly and patted her on the shoulder. "Nothing to worry about. I doubt if he chased you. Wolves don't usually attack humans." He led her toward the library and motioned for her to sit down. Then he went over to the portable bar and poured her a shot of brandy. "Here, drink this. It will make you stop shivering."

Bonnie complied, downing the brandy in one gulp, grateful for the warmth that instantly seeped through her. "So, you've seen the wolf before?" she asked as her father poured himself a drink and sat down in the chair across from hers.

"Many times. He's a renegade who shows up every once in a while."

"A renegade?"

Walter nodded. "A wolf without a family, without a pack."

Bonnie nodded absently, thinking of that moment when her gaze had met the wolf's. There had been an instant of connection, a strange feeling of familiarity, a long second when she felt as if they were both very old souls meeting in a new lifetime.

She shook her head, dismissing the crazy thoughts.

"I thought I'd take a few minutes away from my work to sit and talk with you," Walter said. "I know I've been a poor host since you've arrived and I know you have things you want to talk about."

She leaned forward eagerly, all thoughts of the wolf and his menace evaporating as she realized that she finally had the opportunity to answer some of the questions that had always plagued her about her father. She hesitated, suddenly not knowing where to begin. "I...I just always wondered why you didn't divorce Mom, why you remained married to her, but apart from her."

"I loved your mother," he answered without hesitation. "She was always the only woman for me. Divorce was never an issue." He leaned back in the chair and took another sip of his drink. "She understood the importance of my work. She understood that there wasn't room in my life for two obsessions."

"But what about me? Didn't you ever wonder how I was doing? What I was doing? Didn't you ever want to come and see me?" Bonnie blushed, realizing she sounded like a needy child. She'd thought she'd long ago come to terms with the fatherless child she'd been, but apparently that wasn't so.

"Your mother sent me long letters about you. She also sent pictures."

"That's right. Lauretta told me you always carried a picture of mother and me in your wallet. Can I see it?"

Walter sighed with regret and shook his head. "That particular picture got so old and faded, I finally had to throw it away." Bonnie sighed in disappointment. "However, I do have a photo album here." He arose from his chair and went over to one of the book-laden shelves. He pulled a large plaid-covered album down and handed it to her.

Bonnie opened it eagerly, her heart twisting pain-fully as the first picture she looked at was one of her mother. It had been taken when she was a young woman and her eyes shone with hope for the future. The next picture was again of Bonnie's mother, this time holding a baby in her arms. Bonnie flipped the pages of the album slowly, studying each picture in turn, surprised to see so many photos portraying her growing-up years. Her second-grade picture, the one she hated because her mother had given her a frizzy home perm the day before. One of her riding a pony at the county fair. There she was looking stiff and formal as she went to her first school dance. Every major event in her life had been captured on celluloid and placed in the album.

She smiled sadly as one particular picture caught her attention. She had been about four, and it had been taken right after her father had moved out of the house. She had her arm around a big, furry white mutt. Jackemo...yes, that had been the dog's name. "Remember Jackemo?" she asked.

Walter frowned. "Jackemo?"

"Don't you remember?" Bonnie pressed. "Our dog." When there was no flicker of recognition in his eyes, she continued. "He was big and white, an indefinable mixed breed."

"Ah yes, I seem to have some vague recollection," Walter said.

Not for the first time, Bonnie felt a twinge of sadness at her father's answer. What she remembered as important and what he remembered as important seemed to be from two separate lifetimes that had no connections. How could he have only vague recollections of Jackemo? In Bonnie's memories, he and the dog had been inseparable. Images flashed through her head—her father feeding scraps to the eager dog beneath the table; sitting in a chair in the living room, the dog in his lap; the two of them running in circles in the backyard to entertain Bonnie as she laughed in delight.

The dog had died a month after her father had left them. "Just mourned himself to death," her mother had said sadly. So how could he not remember the dog?

Walter smiled at her, as if in apology. "You must forgive me, my dear. Time has a way of erasing things from your memory bank." He smiled beguilingly. "Especially when you get in the advanced stages of age."

Bonnie laughed. "You're hardly ready for a nursing home."

"Ah, but there are times I can't remember the silliest things." Again he smiled with charm. "I guess I'm the epitome of the absent-minded scientist."

She smiled warmly. Perhaps the memories of the past weren't important, she thought. Maybe the only really important thing was the memories they were building together now. "I'm glad I came."

Walter's eyes brightened. "My dear, you'll never know how pleased I am that you are here." His smile transformed to a frown as a loud knock sounded on the front door. "Now, who on earth can that be?"

Mavis walked by the library on her way to the front door. A moment later she stepped into the library, her facial features twisted with worry. "I—I think you'd better come. It's the sheriff."

Walter set his drink on the end table, then left the room, Bonnie following close behind him.

The sheriff was a huge man, well over six feet and equally impressive in breadth. A Neanderthal brow, thick, hanging jowls and a toothpick thrust between his teeth gave him a look of dullness, but from his brown eyes sparked a keen intelligence that Bonnie instantly respected. "You Dr. Redding?" he asked Walter.

"I am. What seems to be the problem?"

Bonnie was vaguely aware of the other men entering the hallway, crowding behind her to find out what was going on. She smiled briefly at Nicholas as he stepped through them and stood near her father, a frown pulling his dark eyebrows together.

"We found a cow a little while ago. It was lying in a field not far from here." He maneuvered the toothpick to the other side of his mouth. "It had been mutilated, its guts ripped out. Day before yesterday, a horse was found in the same condition. Somebody remembered something about a crazy monkey not long ago and thought maybe one of your experimental animals got loose again."

"That's impossible," Bonnie exclaimed. "There are no lab animals here anymore."

The sheriff looked at her, then back at Walter. "Is that a fact?"

Walter nodded. "We stopped using animals in our experiments several months ago."

"Maybe it was the wolf," Bonnie interjected, remembering the fierce, hungry look of the creature she'd encountered.

"Wolf?" Again the sheriff looked at her with interest.

She nodded. "I saw a huge one this afternoon out in the woods."

The sheriff frowned. "Are you sure it was a wolf? We haven't had any reports of those in these parts for years."

"I'm positive." Bonnie shivered, remembering the gleam of the wolf's eyes, the sharp canine teeth that had gnashed together as if in anticipation.

"I don't know," the sheriff said, spitting his toothpick out on the ground. "A wolf would have attacked the cow because of hunger, but that cow wasn't eaten...it was just ripped apart."

Like the raccoon, Bonnie thought, remembering the mutilated animal Jimmy had found a few days before. She recalled how the forest made her feel, as if some evil entity dwelled there. What was it? What was attacking animals and tearing them apart? She looked over at Nicholas, noting that his face was pale, his jaw muscles working overtime as they clenched and unclenched.

"Well, Sheriff, I don't see how we can help you any further. You can assure the people of Hollow Rock that whatever is killing the animals didn't come from my lab," Walter said.

The sheriff nodded and backed away from the front door. "I'm sorry to bother you folks, but I've got to check out any leads."

Walter nodded, and as the sheriff walked back out to his patrol car, he closed the front door. For a moment they all stood in the hallway, looking at each other. Bonnie felt a tension between them, a tension born of secrets she didn't understand. She didn't understand the look that passed between her father and Nicholas. She didn't understand why Nicholas looked so tense. And more than anything, she didn't understand why the other three scientists looked at Nicholas with fear and accusation.

CHAPTER SEVEN

Bonnie awakened suddenly, unsure what had pulled her from her peaceful sleep. Her room was pitch-black, the fire that had burned earlier now dead in the grate. She'd pulled the heavy draperies across the windows before going to bed, and now not even a sliver of moonlight peeked in to relieve the darkness.

She remained unmoving, trying to discern what exactly had disturbed her. Without the fire, the room was chilly, but not unpleasantly so. She turned her head slightly as she heard first one voice, then another.

She sat up and looked at the luminous dial of her clock. Almost two o'clock. What on earth were her father and Mavis doing arguing in the middle of the night?

Without making a sound, she slid out of the bed and tiptoed over to her bedroom door. She opened it slightly and listened. The voices were louder now, obviously argumentative, but the words were muted enough so that she couldn't discern what was being said.

She stepped back from her door as her father's flew open and Mavis stepped out into the hallway. The older woman was clad in a filmy nightgown, revealing a surprisingly attractive figure. As Bonnie watched, Mavis leaned back into her father's bedroom and said something else before closing Walter's door. Then she stomped down the hallway and on down the stairs.

Bonnie closed her door, thoughts whirling around in her head. When she'd discovered that Jonathon was Jimmy's father, she'd dismissed the idea of Walter and Mavis being lovers. After all, the scientist now resting in the grave in the backyard had only been dead a couple of months. But now she couldn't ignore the fact that it was obvious her father and Mavis were lovers. Why else would the woman be leaving his room in the middle of the night clad only in a sexy nightgown?

Okay, so he's a normal, healthy man, she said to herself as she leaned heavily against the bedroom door. *So he's human.* But even telling herself all this…it still hurt. *He's not a saint,* she thought, remembering Nicholas's words concerning her view of Walter. A piece of her childhood adoration for her father split away and dissolved into the air, unable to exist beneath the weight of reality.

She wasn't angry to discover that her father hadn't stayed faithful to her mother, she was merely saddened by the choices each had made. Her father had been obsessed with his science, and her mother had been obsessed with him. And the sad part of it all was that Bonnie realized neither of them could have been happy. Her father should have divorced her mother, allowed her to find another love, one who would have given her a lifetime of happiness rather than a handful of old memories.

Knowing sleep would be impossible with her mind whirling, she walked over to the window and pulled the draperies open. Twisting the lock on the balcony door, she opened it and stepped outside.

The night wind was wild, whipping her hair around her head like Medusa's snakes. Night clouds skittered across in front of the moon, creating an illumination that wavered and danced as it spilled to the forest floor.

She wrapped her arms around herself, knowing she should go back inside and put on her robe, but the wind stirred something inside her. She raised her face and closed her eyes, enjoying the bracing air that caressed her body.

A branch snapped someplace nearby and she heard the whisper of footsteps against the dry grass near her balcony. She opened her eyes and saw Nicholas.

He stood at the edge of the woods, his eyes reflecting the moonlight and sending it back up to her. He didn't move, but merely stood staring up at her, as if she were a dream image he didn't quite believe was really there. She raised her hand to acknowledge his presence.

She suddenly realized that the breeze pressed her thin nightgown intimately against her body, molding it to her every curve. The silver glint in his gaze seemed to intensify, and Bonnie felt a deep heat begin to form in the pit of her stomach. Desire…it radiated from him in waves, sending its energy to her with an electrical sizzle that seemed to resound in her ears. The heat inside her increased, and she no longer felt the play of the chill wind. Instead, the heat of a desert wind filled her up.

Wordlessly, he summoned her, the expression in his gaze compelling her toward him. She didn't think of refusing the magnetic pull that caused her to leave the balcony and slip soundlessly out of her room. As she moved lightly down the stairs, she felt as if she were in a dream, and suddenly she remembered her erotic dream of him, and she wanted it to be a reality. She wanted to feel his strong arms wrapped around her, keeping her disturbing thoughts of her father at bay. She wanted to lose herself in the glow of his eyes, the heat of his body, the mystery of his soul.

She opened the door that led outside, the night air once again caressing her flesh, whipping her gown around her knees. She looked at the place where she had seen him, frowning as she saw only the shadowed depths of the night. Had he been there at all? Had he only been a figment of her imagination?

"You shouldn't have come." Nicholas spoke from behind her, watching as she twirled around, her green eyes widened in a mixture of surprise and pleasure.

She moved toward him, bringing with her the scent

that so stirred his blood. "I wasn't sure you were real." She stood so close to him her breath was a soft whisper against his neck. "I thought...I thought you might be a part of my dreams."

He closed his eyes, knowing he should send her back to the safety of her room, knowing he should be smart and run as far away from her as possible. But he didn't want to be smart, not tonight. He was tired of being smart and doing what he thought was right.

For just this moment in time, he wanted to forget who he was, what he was, and just exist in the clear depths of her eyes. He wanted to feel the softness of her body pressed against his. He longed to caress the richness of her hair and see her eyes darken with hunger for him. For just this instant of eternity, he wanted to be a normal man and make love to Bonnie.

He battled with his choices, feeling as if his soul were ripping apart.

"Nicholas?"

He felt the softness of her hand as she reached up and stroked the side of his face. He opened his eyes and looked at her and knew he was lost. His decision had been made with his heart, not with his head.

With a small groan he gathered her into his arms, covering her lips with his. She tasted of sweet innocence and wild fires and he wanted to lose himself in her forever.

She clung to him, responding to the ravenous hunger of his mouth against hers. Tasting her fire only increased the flames that burned inside him.

He moved his hands across the small of her back, reveling first in the feel of the cool silk of her gown, then the contrast of the heat of her skin beneath.

"Nicholas..." She pulled slightly away from him, taking his hands in hers. "Come with me.... Come to my room and make love to me." Her eyes shone with promise, a sensual expectation deepening their springlike hue.

He felt dazed, realizing that had she not broken their embrace he would have taken her here, on the concrete patio. Yet the thought of making love to her in the cursed house, in the room right next to Walter's, filled him with revulsion. Nor could he take her to his own room, where he feared his hidden secrets would spin her into insanity. No, instead he wanted her in his secret place, in the retreat he'd found deep in the cave, a place far removed from the evils of the institute. He wanted her in his lair.

"No...come with me." He gently pulled on her hand, leading her toward the dense darkness of the woods. As she went with him unquestioningly, obviously trusting him implicitly, his heart swelled within his chest, causing a curiously tight sensation that was both frightening and wonderful at the same time. It was a sensation he'd never experienced before.

Deeper and deeper they went into the woods, neither of them saying a word. As the trees overhead absorbed the moonlight, the darkness grew profound, but Nicholas's uncanny night vision led them unerringly to the cave entrance.

Once there, he reached just inside and withdrew a flashlight. He turned it on, the beam a near-futile effort against the utter blackness within.

He walked her through the narrow passageway, into the large cavern, sensing her surprise when he didn't stop but rather continued on, following the stream as it meandered into the back recesses of the cave.

"Nicholas?" Her voice held no fear, only curiosity.

"Shhh," he replied, squeezing her hand in assurance. He felt a strange sense of inevitability, a rightness to them being here together, and he wasn't sure if it came only from his intense desire for her or if fate itself had decreed this single moment in time.

As he entered the small room at the back of the cave, he wondered briefly if he should have brought her here. This was his space, the place he came to when the weight of the institute pressed on him, when the horror of the demons inside him threatened to consume him in despair. He'd only allowed Jimmy to share this secret place with him, knowing that Jimmy would never betray him, that the boy wanted only friendship and respect from him. And what did Bonnie want from him? That was a question yet to be answered.

He lit the kerosene lantern, turning to see Bonnie's expression of surprise as the flickering illumination spilled around the room. He followed her gaze, as if viewing the cozy room through her eyes. The mattress on the floor was ancient, covered with a faded patchwork quilt that did little to hide its lumpy condition. The table near the bed was old and scarred, holding the kerosene lantern, a deck of cards and a vase full of withering wildflowers. He looked at her, unsure what to expect from her. She walked over to the vase of flowers, touching a near-dead blossom with the tip of her finger. "Jimmy brought the flowers here, didn't he?"

Nicholas nodded, feeling his blood pound ferociously in his temples as she sat down on the mattress and smiled up at him, a smile of promise. Her hair was wildly tousled, her cheeks a bright blush of pink. The nightgown clung to her, emphasizing the delicacy of her collarbones, the creamy swell of her breasts. Her nipples were already erect in anticipation.

A dull roaring began in his head as he moved toward her, wanting to lose himself in the green depths of her eyes, dwell only in the sweet spring scent of her. He joined her on the mattress, his arms enfolding her as together they sank down into the folds of the quilt.

His lips found hers in a kiss that was at first gentle and explorative. He tasted the sweetness, savored the texture of her mouth against his. With deliberate slowness, he deepened the kiss, his tongue first tracing the swell of her lower lip, then dipping inside to tease and torment.

As he kissed her, her fingers worked frantically to unbutton his shirt, as if she couldn't wait to feel his bare flesh. This thought only fed the hunger that flamed in his soul. He withdrew from the kiss only long enough to shrug out of his shirt, then pulled her to him again, reveling in the feel of her silk-covered breasts pressed intimately against his heated chest.

Suddenly he was impatient with the material that remained as a barrier between them. With a groan, he unsnapped his pants and slid them off, then in one fluid motion, grabbed the end of her nightgown and pulled it over her head. He threw it across the small room, where it landed on the floor in a luminous puddle of white.

For an endless moment they merely looked into one another's eyes, Nicholas feeling as if he were drowning in the raw emotion that emanated from hers. It was passion, it was desire…but it was also something more, and it was that something more that made him want to lose himself in her forever.

He rolled over on top of her, his mouth once again seeking hers in a kiss less gentle as intense hunger ripped through him. She responded with a hunger of her own, first tangling her hands in his hair, then moving them down to explore the contours of his back. She pressed intimately against him, letting him know she was immediately ready for him, but he held himself back, wanting to savor each caress, give them both enough pleasure to last a lifetime.

He rained kisses down her face, nibbling and biting the sweet skin of her jaw, the tender area of her neck, lingering at her breasts, where he kissed first one, then the other erect tip. The scent of her skin whipped his senses into frenzied need, the taste of her driving him to fight consciously for tenuous control.

He would have been able to maintain a certain modicum of control had she not arched against him and moaned his name. But the moment he heard her impassioned whisper, the moment he felt her so soft, so yielding, his control snapped.

With a guttural moan, he took her, sliding into her warmth with a force that shook them both. For a moment his heart stopped, and he feared he'd hurt her, but as he gazed down into her eyes, he saw a lustful wildness that matched the one that raged inside him.

Time and space lost all meaning as Nicholas moved within her, losing himself to a sensation more intense than any he'd experienced. As her legs wrapped around his hips, drawing him deeper, closer, his thrusts increased in intensity and he drew them into a vortex of passion that threatened to consume them both.

Suddenly he was there, vaguely aware of her cries of release as he stiffened against her, shuddering in his own climax. Almost immediately he rolled off her, drawing her against his side as close as physically possible.

Bonnie nestled against him, awed by the myriad of emotions that swept through her. This strange man, with his dark secrets and deep mysteries, had touched her as no other had before, and she had a feeling no other ever would. She hardly knew him at all, feared the part he kept so well guarded, but despite this, she was falling in love with him.

This thought filled her with enormous joy and incredible fear. Who was this man with his silvery eyes, whom the others eyed suspiciously, who had loved her so completely and now held her so gently?

She ran a hand through the thick matting of hair on his chest, feeling the rhythmic pulse of his heartbeat beneath her palm. The beating of his heart reassured her that he was simply a man...a man who needed to be loved.

"I've never made love to a woman who wanted nothing from me." His voice was soft, reflecting the awe she herself felt.

Bonnie raised her head and smiled at him. "And have you made love to a lot of women?"

"No...only two." He answered with a blunt honesty that surprised her. "One was a scientist who wanted to work on a particular project with me. At the time, I didn't know that was what she was after. The other one was a teacher who wanted to take my mind and control it." His gaze searched her face, and

Bonnie had the distinct feeling that his mind was probing hers, calculating, assessing. His body stiffened slightly, almost imperceptibly. "So what is it you want from me?"

She looked at him in surprise. "Nothing... absolutely nothing," she replied softly, feeling his muscles once again relax at her answer. She lay her head back down, watching the flickering shadows dancing on the cave wall. "What exactly is this place?"

"It's just my place," he answered. "It's where I come when I need to be completely alone."

There had been a moment of apprehension when he'd led her through the large cavern and toward the back of the cave, but the moment Bonnie had entered this smaller room, she'd known it was Nicholas's special place and her tinge of anxiety had passed. The room smelled of him, a wild scent that was at once intriguing, compelling.

Now, thinking back to that moment when she'd stood on the balcony and looked down at him, she couldn't remember when she'd made the decision to make love to him. She only knew that when she'd stood there and seen his eyes shining with desire, she'd been unable to do anything but respond. Even now, the walk through the dark woods to the cave was lost in a haze of inevitability. She wasn't sure now if she had made the decision to make love to him, or if the decision had been made for her by some power greater than them both.

She smiled as she remembered her erotic dream of him. As vivid as the dream had been, the fantasy images didn't begin to compare with the reality of making love to Nicholas. She wanted to ask him so many things. She wanted to know if it had been as wonderful, as special for him as it had been for her. She wanted to ask him if he, too, had felt the strange inevitability in their being here together. But she realized his breathing was deep and slow and the arms that held her close had slackened. She raised her head and looked at him. He was asleep.

She studied his face, the flickering lantern light giving it a haunting beauty. In repose, his face was still lean, retaining an aura of strength, but the torment was gone, the tension dissipated. His jawline was darkened with the new growth of whiskers, and Bonnie remembered the erotic feel of his slightly scratchy cheeks against her skin. She flushed, realizing she already wanted him again. Instead of following through on this new burst of desire, she lay her head back down and regulated her breathing to his.

Nicholas awoke, instantly alert, as always, to his surroundings. One arm was numb, trapped beneath Bonnie's body as she slept soundly at his side. He let it remain there, unwilling to break the embrace that warmed him from the inside out. He didn't want to break the spell that had been spun around them, like a spiderweb keeping them captive in each other's arms.

He stared at her, taking in every minute detail of her loveliness. He wanted to live his life in her eyes, breathe his air from the echo of her gentle sighs, exist forever in the magic of her arms.

But of course, he knew this was impossible. Eventually reality had to intrude—and his reality was ugly and savage.

As always, when he thought of what he was, the fact that he might never be normal again, might never lead a normal life, the anger inside him reared its head. And the anger fed the alien genes in his body, causing them to surge with blood, creating the familiar, dreaded tingling that began in his stomach and radiated outward.

Dear God, not now, he begged, trying to tamp down the anger that swirled inside him. But its hold was too great, and the searing heat that always prefaced his transformation engulfed his body. His head pounded in a rhythm he thought would surely drive him mad.

It was too late to run, too late to get Bonnie to safety. She lay vulnerable beside him, blissfully unaware of the subtle changes now occurring in him.

Nicholas closed his eyes, beads of sweat popping up on the surface of his skin as he fought against the change that would steal his humanity and plunge him into the darkness of unconscious evil. The change brought with it a complete disintegration of the soul, a blackness fearful in its profoundness.

He was vaguely conscious of Bonnie stirring restlessly against him. *Don't wake up,* he silently begged her. *Don't open your eyes and look at me.*

As he felt the subtle shifting of his bones and muscles, felt the lengthening of fingernails into claws, he prayed that she wouldn't awaken to see the nightmare he was becoming, for he knew it would be the image she carried with her in death.

Desperately, he gulped in huge breaths of air, his body trembling from the strain of trying to fight off the insidious alien state. He focused on Bonnie, on the shiny strands of her blond hair, the clear, innocent depths of her green eyes. He replayed in his mind their bodies moving together, united in spirit for that moment in time when their heartbeats had beat as one. He held that image in his mind like a talisman, concentrating on the wonder of their act of making love.

Surprisingly, his anger began to recede. The heat within him lost some of its intensity, causing him to shudder as the energy slowly drained out of his body. He felt his bones, his muscles reshifting, returning to their normal state. He choked back tears of relief, realizing he'd beaten it this time...but what about the next?

He looked at the woman sleeping next to him. He'd

been a fool to chance this…to bring her here, to spend time alone with her.

He shuddered as he thought of what might have happened. Had he not been able to control the raging beast within, he would have ripped her throat out, torn her sweet flesh apart.

He'd allowed himself a momentary respite from reality, but it was a single moment that would not, could not, be repeated. He'd been a fool to risk it once, but he feared he'd be a murderer if he allowed it to happen again.

The anger of only moments before was now completely gone, leaving behind only a void within him that filled with a dull hopelessness.

"Bonnie…" He roused her gently, allowing his hand to linger over the silky smoothness of her shoulder. "Bonnie, wake up. I have to take you back now."

She stirred and opened her eyes, smiling at him, a smile that tore at his heart, ripped apart his insides. "I just want to stay right here with you," she said, snuggling closer against his side.

"You can't stay here," he said, rising from the mattress and reaching for her nightgown. He tossed it to her, then grabbed his slacks and slipped them on, urgent in the need to get her out of here and back to the safety of her room.

She pulled the gown over her head, and he reached out his hand to help her up off the mattress. As he pulled her up, she came into the circle of his arms, and for just a moment he allowed himself one last moment to breathe in her sweet scent, feel her warmth pressed against him. He memorized her presence, drinking of her essence. He finally broke the embrace, taking her hand and silently leading her out of the small room and through the cave.

As he took her through the forest, Bonnie realized they must have been asleep for some time. The illumination of dawn blazed red and gold streaks in the eastern skies, somewhat alleviating the darkness of night and promising another beautiful fall day. The promise of a bright new day was not only in the sunrise, but it also beat in Bonnie's heart as she remembered the passion she and Nicholas had shared. There was something real, something magical between the two of them, and she knew that no matter how things turned out between herself and her father, Nicholas would be there for her. It was a comforting thought, one that eased the loneliness that had plagued her since her mother's death.

As they reached the patio, he turned to her, his eyes dark and fathomless. "Bonnie." Her name was a sigh of torture, and she sensed that he somehow regretted what they had shared. After all, he worked for her father...and hated him. It was no wonder he felt torn about what had transpired between them.

"Shhh." She reached up and lay her fingers against his lips, then tilted her head up and replaced her fingers with her mouth. He held himself stiff, unyielding, for a long moment, then with a groan he gathered her against him and returned her kiss with an intensity that left her gasping.

"Good night," she finally whispered reluctantly, then turned to go back to her room.

When she got back upstairs, she went immediately to her balcony and saw him still standing on the patio below. Their gazes locked, held for an infinity, and again Bonnie felt a connection that transcended space and time, here and now. He finally broke the connection, turning and disappearing back into the woods in the direction from which they had come.

With a sigh, Bonnie turned and left the balcony, stifling a yawn with the back of her hand. She turned on her bedside lamp, then walked over to the mirror and stared at her reflection, the memory of Nicholas's kisses, his caresses, bringing a flush of pleasure to her cheeks.

She didn't understand the mysteries that lived here at the institute, but Nicholas's soul was not one of the mysteries. As she thought of his gentleness, the warm strength of his arms surrounding her, she knew with a certainty she had nothing to fear from him.

She frowned suddenly and moved closer to the mirror, her gaze noticing something on the bodice of her gown. Her frown deepened. A hair. She picked it off and held it between two fingers, noticing others clinging to the silk of her gown. They weren't from her, and they weren't from Nicholas. These were about three inches long, and gray…and very coarse, like dog hair.

She stared at the one between her fingers, a shiver of horror sweeping through her like a cold arctic wind. Where had they come from? Had some animal been in the cave, watching silently as she and Nicholas had made love? No, not some animal…the wolf. The hairs looked like they had come from the wolf she had seen in the woods. The thought filled her with a sick revulsion and a terrifying fear.

Why would there be wolf hairs in the cave? Wouldn't the wolf be afraid to enter a place that so obviously contained the human scent?

Where did Nicholas fit in with all this? Did he know the wolf had been in his area of the cave? What connection was there between Nicholas and the wolf she'd seen in the woods? The questions came fast and furious, and with them the knowledge that Nicholas was as much a mystery as everything else in this house. She might be in love with him, but there was a part of her that wondered if she shouldn't leave this place, forget getting closer to her father and run from the closeness she felt with Nicholas.

She thought of the sheriff's visit, and her heart pounded anxiously. Yes, Nicholas had been right. There was evil here, but what she didn't know was whether she should warn Nicholas or run from him.

CHAPTER EIGHT

She had no idea how long she stood in front of the mirror, staring at the hairs that clung to her nightgown. Wolf hairs... She couldn't seem to stop shivering.

She finally changed into a clean gown and climbed into bed, her sleep plagued with strange dreams of nightmare creatures and ferocious wolves, of Nicholas Shepherd and bizarre experiments.

She awoke more exhausted than she'd been when she'd fallen asleep. It wasn't a physical exhaustion, but rather a mental one more draining than mere body tiredness.

Her father and Mavis...herself and Nicholas... mutilated animals, renegade wolves... It all swirled around in her head in dizzying confusion.

Pulling herself out of bed, she went into the bathroom and ran a tub of hot water. Easing herself into the warmth, she relaxed, closing her eyes and allowing her mind to replay the lovemaking she and Nicholas had shared the night before. That, at least, was clear in her mind, vivid in detail with no whispering dark edges to muddle the memory.

It had been like nothing she had experienced before in her life. The intensity of her response to him had been unbelievable. She frowned, picking up the sponge from the side of the tub. She remembered his words about his two previous relationships with women who'd only wanted to crawl into his head, but wanted nothing to do with his soul. How sad.

Finishing her bath, she dressed quickly, anxious to find Nicholas. She wanted to talk to him about the strange hairs she'd found the night before. She'd decided that the only logical explanation was that the huge gray wolf had at one time been in the cave... long before Nicholas had claimed the area as his own. Surely the hairs were merely remnants of the wolf's previous visit and nothing more. Certainly this made more sense than any other scenario her brain could conjure.

Feeling infinitely better, she ran lightly down the stairs to the dining room, where Mavis was clearing breakfast dishes from the table.

"Good morning," she greeted the older woman, fighting against a fleeting tinge of resentment as she thought of the housekeeper and her father together. "Have you seen Nicholas this morning?"

"He's down in the lab. Went down there just after daybreak and didn't come up with the others for breakfast."

Bonnie nodded and went over to the buffet and poured herself a cup of coffee. Since Bonnie often slept later than the men, Mavis had taken to putting the coffee here, where she could help herself. She sat down at the table and watched as Mavis finished her cleaning. "You don't like Nicholas very well, do you?"

Mavis's eyes widened slightly, then darkened like draperies pulled tightly across a window. "It's not my place to like or dislike," she finally answered grudgingly.

"But surely you have an opinion about him," Bonnie pressed.

"I have an opinion, but I learned a long time ago that my opinions don't count for much. Like whistles in the wind, nobody hears them and nobody cares. And that's all you'll get from me." She compressed her lips tightly, picked up her tray of dirty dishes and disappeared through the swinging doors into the kitchen.

Bonnie released a heavy sigh, wondering why it was that no matter what she asked, she couldn't get a straight answer from anyone. Everybody talked in riddles—everyone but Jimmy who couldn't talk at all. She smiled at thoughts of the copper-headed boy, wondering what he was doing on this cloudy morning.

She wondered if Mavis knew how much time Jimmy spent with Nicholas? Somehow she didn't think Mavis would approve of the friendship between the dark, mysterious man and the freckle-faced boy.

She looked at her watch, wondering how long Nicholas would be down in the lab. Surely she'd get an opportunity to talk to him sometime this afternoon or this evening. With this thought in mind, she sipped her coffee and wondered how she was going to spend the long hours of the day.

However, she didn't see Nicholas that afternoon or evening. In fact, for the next three days she didn't see him at all. It was as if he'd moved down to the lab. As far as she knew, he didn't come up for meals, nor did he leave the basement to sleep. And with each day that passed, Bonnie grew more and more anxious to see him, talk to him...afraid that he was intentionally putting distance between them in an attempt to deny the night they had shared.

As frustrating was the fact that her father seemed equally obsessed with his work, avoiding Bonnie's attempts to spend time with him. She found herself wondering again and again why he had finally agreed to allow her to come here if he didn't want to spend time with her.

She spent her days pouring over the photo albums with its pictures of her mother and herself, disappointed that there were none of her father in the faded pages. She turned to the back pages...empty pages that held evidence that photos had once been there. She wondered what pictures had been in these back pages, why they had been removed.

In the afternoons, she helped Jimmy weed around the birdbath, always with an eye to the woods, not wanting to be taken by surprise by the huge wolf who had frightened her so badly before.

"Nicholas is certainly working long hours," she observed that evening when she and the others were all eating supper.

"Nicholas often goes on work binges," her father observed. "Other times days will go by when he doesn't touch the equipment or come near the lab."

"It can't be healthy to work such hours. Is he eating or sleeping at all?"

Walter paused, his fork halfway to his mouth. "Such concern for Nicholas…. Have I missed something here?"

Bonnie felt the blush that covered her face, and her father's smile widened. "It would seem that I have." He laughed in obvious delight, the other men at the table merely looking uncomfortable. "I'd rather hoped you and Nicholas would become close. Tell me, have you slept with him yet?"

"Father!" Bonnie felt her blush become a flame of embarrassment.

Walter grimaced. "I suppose that was rather insensitive of me, wasn't it. I'm afraid this father business is still a bit new to me and it's only natural I'm going to make mistakes." He smiled charmingly. "I suppose it's just my scientific brain at work…. I was merely after the facts of the situation."

Bonnie nodded, still shocked by her father's inappropriate question. She had heard of women who had very open relationships with their parents, but she wasn't ready for this kind of openness with her father. He had yet to learn what her favorite color was, her favorite food. She certainly wasn't comfortable enough with him to share with him the details of her sexual activities.

"Anyway," Walter continued, "I assure you, my dear, Nicholas has the constitution of an animal. A little sleep and food deprivation won't harm him."

Although the conversation immediately changed, throughout the remainder of the meal, Bonnie continued to feel uncomfortable. The inappropriateness of her father's question merely pointed out the wide chasm that existed between father and daughter, the unnatural aspect of their relationship.

Following dinner, Bonnie went into the library and poked at the fire that someone had lit. The day had been gray and overcast, and thunder had rumbled as they'd finished the meal.

There was a storm moving in, and Bonnie almost welcomed it. She felt a storm brewing within her. Perhaps nature's display of electricity and power would somehow relieve the pressure building in her.

She put the poker back in its stand, then walked over to the window and stared outside. Already storm winds whipped the trees into a frenzy, sending brown, withered leaves twirling and swirling in the air. Lightning flashed in the distance and several moments later the thunder replied.

Once again Bonnie was struck by the aura of strangeness that permeated the forest. It was nothing she could quite put her finger on. There were no alien plants, no mutated flowers to indicate something amiss. The trees weren't any more gnarled or twisted than in any other forest.

So, what was it about this particular wooded area that sent a chill up her spine? What was it that made her feel that something was profoundly wrong here?

The answer suddenly popped into her head. The animals... Yes, of course. It was the utter absence of animals that bothered her. Other than the mutilated raccoon Jimmy had found, and the large wolf that had confronted her, she'd not seen a single, solitary creature. No squirrels scurried among the tree limbs, foraging nuts and grains for the approaching winter. No rabbits hopped about seeking sites for new burrows.

Although there were birds, there seemed to be no nests, as if the winged creatures found the forest fine to fly through, but not a place to build a permanent home.

"A nice place to visit, but I wouldn't want to live here," Bonnie murmured aloud, echoing what she thought were the birds' sentiments. *I should leave here,* she thought, turning away from the window and flopping down in one of the chairs. She should go back home, get on with her life. She should just leave, forget about her father and this place.

But even as she entertained the idea, there was one

thing that made her reluctant to go immediately upstairs and pack her bags.

Nicholas. His name sang through her heart and she knew it would be very difficult to forget the haunting shadows of his eyes, the gentleness of his lovemaking. She couldn't leave him...not yet. She needed to allow this new love she had for him to finish blossoming, she needed to give them both time to discover what magical place their feelings would take them to. She just couldn't turn her back on him and walk away.

She sighed and shifted her position in her chair. What she wanted to do more than anything at this moment was talk to Nicholas. She wanted to find out what was running through his troubled mind. Was he intentionally avoiding her? Hiding out in the lab because of his regret about making love to her? How could he? How could he possibly regret something that beautiful, something that had felt so good and right?

She noticed that from where she sat, she had a perfect vantage point of the stairway that led down to the lab. She realized if she sat in this very chair long enough, eventually she would see Nicholas when he came upstairs. And sooner or later, he would have to leave the lab. She settled back, gaze locked on the stairway, willing to wait as long as it took.

Bonnie still sat there long after midnight. The other men had come up and gone to bed and the house was quiet except for the occasional flashes of lightning and the distant roll of thunder from the passing storm.

She considered venturing downstairs to the lab, but dismissed the idea, reluctant to go into the scientists' domain without invitation.

Several times as she waited, she got up to add another log to the fire. She had no lights on in the room, but enjoyed the soft glow and warmth of the brightly burning flames.

She had almost nodded off to sleep when she heard heavy footsteps coming up the stairs from the lab. She immediately straightened in the chair, her heart thudding anxiously in her chest as her gaze locked hungrily on the doorway. And then he was there.

For a moment he didn't see her, and she watched as he leaned wearily against the doorframe, closed his eyes and ran his hand through his hair as if the climb up the stairs had completely exhausted him.

Bonnie's heart reached out toward him and his eyes flickered open as if he felt her presence. He turned his head and looked at her, swift desire darkening his eyes for a moment. Then, almost as quickly, weary resignation tightened his jaw.

"It's very late. What are you doing still up?" he asked quietly, joining her in the room.

"Waiting for you," she answered simply.

He sighed tiredly and sank down into the chair

across from hers. He stared into the fire, the flickering light deepening the lines of exhaustion on his face.

He looked into the flames with a deep concentration, and Bonnie sensed that whatever work had kept him down in the lab for three days and nights hadn't completely released him yet.

She sat patiently, waiting for his mind to resurface from wherever it had gone. After a long moment, he blinked several times, ran his hand through his hair, then turned and looked at her, his eyes holding a weary resignation.

"If I didn't know any better, I'd swear you have been avoiding me." She spoke quickly before he had a chance to say anything. "It isn't very gentlemanly to spend the night with a woman, make love to her, then ignore her very existence." She tried to keep her voice light and teasing, but knew there was an undertone of hurt she couldn't control.

He smiled, an unpleasant one that did nothing to alleviate the darkness of his expression, the tension in his face. "What ever made you think I was a gentleman?" he countered.

"Nicholas...don't."

"Don't what?"

Bonnie got up from her chair and walked over to him. She knelt in front of him, placing her hands on his strong thighs, enjoying the feel of his firm muscles beneath the denim jeans.

He flinched, stiffening as if in defense against her

touch. "Don't cheapen it," she said softly. "Please, don't make something ugly out of what was so beautiful, so right."

"So right?" The explosion came swiftly, unexpectedly from him. He jumped up out of the chair and swept past her, stalking to the fireplace where he gripped the mantel, his back rigid as his knuckles turned white. "Bonnie, it wasn't right. It was all wrong." The anger that had lifted him out of the chair was gone, replaced by a defeated hopelessness that tore at Bonnie's heart. He turned back around and faced her, his eyes mirroring the torture of his soul. "It should never have happened, and it definitely won't happen again." His hand trembled as he raked it through his hair once again.

"Nicholas, please, don't make any decisions now, not when you're obviously exhausted." She wasn't willing to accept what he'd said, but neither did she want to argue with him when he was beyond exhaustion.

Besides, she didn't want to fight with him. What she wanted to do was hold him, stroke away the tired lines in his forehead, chase away the shadows from his eyes. She wanted to lie in his arms and whisper her most private fantasies, share with him her most secret dreams.

She did none of these things. Instead she responded to him in the practical way taught to her by her mother. "Why don't you let me fix you something to eat." She stood up and walked over to him, touching him lightly on his shoulder. "Come on. How long has it been since you've had a meal?" He shrugged, and she continued. "How can you think effectively if you can't even remember the last time you've eaten?"

He hesitated a moment, then nodded, and together they went into the kitchen. Nicholas sat down on one of the stools at the wooden work counter, and Bonnie went to the refrigerator to see what she could scrounge up for him.

"We had a delicious baked ham for dinner," she said, rummaging through the covered platters of leftovers. "I'm sure we didn't eat all of it.... Ah, here it is." She pulled the meat out and quickly cut off two generous slabs. "This will make a couple of great sandwiches."

As she found the bread, pulled off some lettuce, then sliced a tomato, she watched Nicholas covertly, realizing that once again he had drifted off into a world she couldn't enter.

When she placed the plate of sandwiches before him, he looked up, as if startled by his surroundings. He smiled in apology as she poured him a tall glass of milk, then joined him at the counter.

He ate hungrily, and Bonnie watched him silently, enjoying the mere sight of him relishing the food.

There was something intimate about sharing the kitchen in the middle of the night. She felt the anxiety

that had plagued her since arriving at the institute fade
beneath the normalcy of watching a man eat a sandwich and drink a glass of milk.

All her disappointment in not being able to connect
with her father was banished as she once again felt a
curious connection being forged with the man who
sat across from her. As she watched him eat, the distant rumble of thunder from the passing storm was
the only sound in the kitchen.

He finished the last of his sandwich, drained the
glass of milk, then smiled at her. "Thanks. I needed
that."

She returned his smile, noting that he did look
slightly refreshed, as if the food had instantly revital-
ized him.

She reached out and covered one of his hands with
hers. For a moment his lay inert beneath hers, neither
accepting nor protesting the touch. Then slowly, he
turned his hand over, allowing their fingers to en-
twine. He closed his eyes, grimacing as if in enormous pain. "Ah, Bonnie…why did you have to come
here?"

She didn't answer, recognizing the question as a
rhetorical one that demanded no reply. She merely
tightened her grip on his fingers, unable to understand
the source of his enormous pain. "Tell me about your
work," she asked softly, wanting him to talk about
anything and everything that was important to him.

"My work?" He sighed, and once again the tired

lines chased each other across his face, deepening his look of weariness. A flash of lightning peeked into the kitchen window, slashing across his face and intensifying its harshness. And although she could see him perfectly, although she held his hand in hers, she knew he had drifted back to the lab. "I'm so close…so close but it's still not right." His voice was a soft whisper of thought. "The formula is still not right." He looked at her unseeingly, his eyes blazing with a feverish light that instantly dimmed when he focused on her again. "It doesn't matter," he finally said. He squeezed her hand tightly, almost hurting her. "Bonnie, I'm begging you. Leave here…tonight, first thing tomorrow…. Leave now."

Bonnie stared at him, realizing that no matter what happened now, she couldn't leave. It had nothing at all to do with her father. It had everything to do with Nicholas. Even though his lips told her to leave, his eyes compelled her to stay.

She slowly shook her head.

Nicholas released his grip on her hand. "Then you'll be as damned as the rest of us here."

"And just what, exactly, does that mean?" she returned, the frustration she'd been battling for days coming swiftly to the surface. He merely sighed heavily, but didn't answer, further fueling Bonnie's irritation. "I am so tired of these enigmatic little statements you calmly drop without any further explanations. My father won't talk to me, you won't talk to me. Jimmy can't talk to me.'' She studied his face searchingly. ''I know there are strange things going on around here. Everyone seems to have secrets. But nobody will share them with me.''

''Trust me, Bonnie. You don't want to know the secrets that surround this place.'' His eyes were darkly shuttered against her, and a small smile curved his lips upward.

He reached out a hand and slowly trailed a finger down the side of her face. His touch evoked a familiar heat deep inside her. Slowly, sensually, he caressed down her cheekbone, across her jawline and over the fullness of her bottom lip. He finally captured her chin between his thumb and forefinger. For a long moment his eyes stared into hers, causing her to catch her breath. Almost imperceptibly, his fingers begin to apply pressure, hurting her with the strength of his grip. ''Stay away from me, Bonnie.'' There was a blatant warning in his tone.

''Why? You could never hurt me,'' she answered in a breathless whisper. ''I know you, Nicholas. I know you would never—could never—hurt me.''

His grip on her chin intensified, tears springing to her eyes as she saw the black abyss of his gaze. ''No one ever knows the true soul of another.'' He released her, pushed away from the counter and stood up. ''I've got several things to clean up down in the lab. Then I need to get some sleep.'' He turned and left the kitchen, heading for the stairway back down to the lab.

As Bonnie watched him go, she released a shuddery sigh, then jumped as she heard another noise…the sound of furtive footsteps moving up the stairway. She scooted off the stool and stepped out of the kitchen, gazing up the darkened stairs. Nothing. There was nothing there but the deep shadows of the night.

Had she imagined the footsteps? She didn't think so. Somebody had run up the stairs. She frowned and rubbed her forehead, feeling the beginning of a headache starting between her eyes. Why would anyone be up at this time of the night? And why would they be eavesdropping on her and Nicholas?

It wasn't until she got into bed that she once again replayed that moment in the kitchen when Nicholas had caressed her face so lovingly, his eyes radiating a savage intensity as frightening as his sudden grip on her chin.

For a moment she'd felt the same sort of frightening fascination that she'd experienced when she'd gazed into the wolf's eyes. Glowing eyes…predatory eyes…animal eyes…Nicholas's eyes… Round and round the images spun in her mind, melding, coalescing until they were all one and the same.

She squeezed her eyes tightly closed, wanting only the peaceful oblivion of sleep to blanket her thoughts and keep her sane…at least until the morning.

CHAPTER NINE

She found the book the next day. It was sitting in the middle of her bed when she came back inside after helping Jimmy weed around the old birdbath. It was a big, black tome, lettered on the front in gold. Curious, she picked it up.

The Curse of the Beast: Legends and Myths of the Werewolf. She read the title with a frown, wondering who had left it here for her.

She sat down on the edge of the bed, shoving a strand of her hair off her forehead as she caressed the gold lettering, then slowly opened it and thumbed through the pages.

As she looked at the black-and-white drawings contained inside, she knew this was not a book to curl up with on a dark and stormy night...nor was it one she'd want to read just before falling asleep. The pictures were various artistic renditions of werewolves, horrible drawings of hairy, fierce-looking creatures in torment.

The drawings were scattered throughout the pages. At the front of the book, they were depictions of werewolves as half man, half beast—walking upright on two legs, just covered with hair and possessing wolflike facial features. Toward the end of the book, they changed, showing the nightmare beasts as wolves...sleek, dangerous and strangely compelling, with gleaming eyes that radiated a cunning, almost human intelligence and a profound evil.

Her frown deepened as she studied the book in her hands. Who had left it here? And why? Why would anyone want her to read a book about werewolves?

Despite the strangeness of finding the book on her bed, her curiosity overwhelmed her. She plumped the pillows behind her, settled back and began to read.

It was nearly two hours later when she surfaced again, her head reeling from all the information the pages had imparted to her. Information she couldn't imagine using unless she found herself on a movie lot with Lon Chaney as her co-star. She smiled, remembering the first time she'd seen that particular movie. It hadn't frightened her; instead she thought it had been rather campy and overplayed.

"Werewolves, indeed," she scoffed, getting off the bed and crossing the room. She opened the balcony door and stepped outside. The storm that had passed the night before had taken the rain with it, but had left behind another dark, gloomy day.

Her smile slowly faded as she gazed at the surrounding woods. If there really was such a thing as werewolves, Bonnie could easily imagine them choosing this place to live.

The area looked especially forbidding today, with the gloom of the clouds overhead giving a gray cast to everything. The light breeze stirred the leaves, causing the whole landscape to subtly seethe, as if the wind were the blood that pumped the heart of an alien entity.

Bits and pieces of what she'd read fluttered around in her brain…werewolves, men doomed to transform into wolves on the night of the full moon, creatures driven by ravenous hungers and torturous rage. According to the legends, it was the curse of the beast to kill those he most loved. Bonnie found a certain haunting sadness in the words of the myth.

And it's my curse to fall in love with a man as dark and mysterious as the woods, she thought as she left the balcony and returned to her room.

Nicholas had been quiet, distant at lunch. He'd refused to meet her gaze, and she'd felt a cold stab of fear as she remembered what he'd said to her the night before, the intensity that had darkened his eyes as he'd held her chin between his fingers.

Surely he hadn't meant it. He would never, ever harm her. Despite his words of warning, she simply couldn't believe that she would ever come to harm because of him. What they had found in each other's arm had been a special kind of magic. She'd felt it and she just knew he'd felt it, too.

She once again stared at the book in the center of the bed, a glaring reminder that all was not right here in her father's house. Who had given it to her? Was it intended as a warning? A threat? Or had somebody merely thought she might find it of interest...a little light reading for those evenings spent alone?

Suddenly she'd had it. The book, with its bizarre content and horrifying pictures, was the last straw. The secrets, the aura of darkness that permeated the place, her father's distance, Nicholas's savage rejection...all of it combined, swirled around and overwhelmed her. She stalked across the room, grabbed the book and pitched it against the wall, satisfied with the resulting resounding thud.

A large lump swelled in her throat, and no matter how hard she swallowed, it wouldn't go away. Tears burned behind her eyes, and in a moment of uncharacteristic weakness, she gave in to the despair.

She shed tears for the mother she'd known and loved, for the father she hardly knew, and finally for Nicholas, the man she'd come to love.

She should leave here. Mavis would be thrilled if she left and it would probably take a week for her father to even realize she'd gone.

And Nicholas...would he be happy to see her go? She truly didn't know. Although his mouth kept telling her to leave, his eyes said something much different. And when he'd held her in his arms, his body had spoken eloquently—he'd definitely not been telling her to go away. She was so confused by him...by everything.

She wiped at her tears, pressing at her temples where a tension headache had begun to pound. She'd come here hoping to fill a void in her heart, a hole she wanted to fill up with her father. Sadly, she would leave with the same empty space, but it was a void she'd learn to live with. She would never begin to understand the man her father was, the choices he had made in his life, but she didn't have to understand, only accept.

She knew that if she left here, she'd never see Nicholas again, and her heart rebelled at the very thought. She loved him, but there was a part of himself he kept secret, a part that somehow frightened her.

She knew he cared about her, too. But what good did it do to love him when he continued to deny that love its very existence?

Yes, it was best to leave now, before she lost any more of her heart to Nicholas. She refused to become like her mother, obsessed with a man who might never be able to return her love.

Eventually, memories of Nicholas would fade, haunting her only in the silent moments of the night when her internal censors were too tired to keep thoughts of him at bay. Yes, the smartest thing to do was to leave as soon as possible.

That night at dinner she told her father her plans to leave the following morning.

"Leave?" He stared at her in disbelief. "Nonsense," he scoffed. "We've hardly had any time together at all. You can't leave yet."

"Father, I've been here nearly two weeks. It's obvious your work takes up most of your time. There's no point in my remaining here any longer." There was no censure in her tone; she was merely stating the facts.

"But you can't leave yet," Walter protested vehemently. He frowned, his mind obviously racing. "I'll tell you what...give me two more days to finish up some of my tabulations down in the lab. Then we'll have a picnic...a full day of celebration." He smiled, warming to his idea. He looked at the other scientists at the table, everyone except Nicholas, who once again hadn't come up from the lab to eat. "Yes, we'll all take off for the day and go down by the pond. It will be a day of relaxation, conversation." He looked at Bonnie, his eyes glittering brightly. "It will be a day for making memories."

Bonnie's resolve to leave the next morning wavered beneath the promise of his words. A day for making memories... It would be wonderful to have some nice memories of her father to take away with her when she left. What possible harm could come from staying a couple more days? she asked herself. And yet there was a small voice inside that urged her to ignore her father's words, pack up and get the hell away from this crazy place. But her desire for those memories was too strong, and when he reached over and patted her hand, she knew she would stay. "Okay...another week," she said, relenting.

"Wonderful," he replied exuberantly, releasing his hold on her hand and returning his attention to the meal.

Almost immediately, Bonnie regretted her decision. How on earth was she going to stand being around Nicholas for another week, seeing him, speaking with him without loving him more deeply every day? Even remembering his cruelty of the night before, despite the fact that something about him frightened her, her heart remained inexplicably bound with his.

It was later that evening that she saw him. She sat in the library, once again thumbing through the book on werewolves, trying to discern why it had been left for her. She hadn't asked anyone about it. It was obvious that whoever had left it hadn't wanted her to know who they were.

She somehow felt that the answers to many of the secrets of the Redding Institute were contained in the text...if she could only figure out the connection. Just holding the book in her hand sent an inexplicable cold chill of apprehension through her.

She looked up as Nicholas came up from the basement. She closed the book and slid it into the cushion next to her as he eased himself down on the chair across from her.

"Walter tells me you were intent on leaving here

in the morning, but he managed to talk you into staying longer.''

Bonnie nodded. ''He's planned a picnic in a couple of days. I figure the extra time won't make that much difference one way or the other.'' She was tense, unsure what to expect from him. It was as if two creatures inhabited his body, the tender, loving man who'd made love to her so gently, and the cruel beast that had gripped her chin so tightly the night before, hurting her as he warned her away from him.

He leaned his head back and closed his eyes, not responding to what she'd said. Once again Bonnie felt that he was battling some internal conflict, and his facial features reflected the torment that obviously twisted his soul.

Soundlessly, she got up from her chair and approached him, kneeling down on the floor beside him, but not touching him in any way. ''Nicholas...talk to me. Let me help you.''

He opened his eyes and looked at her, his gaze full of such emotion, Bonnie felt her heart tearing into tiny pieces. ''You can't help me.'' His voice was a torturous whisper. ''Nobody can help me.'' He reached out his hand and touched a strand of her hair.

Bonnie lay her head on his thigh, and as his hand gently stroked the softness of her hair, she realized it was far too late to save her heart from any more hurt. Nicholas owned her heart. Although she didn't understand his pain, she felt it as if it were her own, and she knew there was no chance of sneaking away from here without leaving a large part of herself behind.

She raised her head, looking into his iridescent green eyes. In one swift movement, before he could protest, she reached up and placed her lips against his. For a moment he held himself still, unyielding to the gentle pressure of her mouth. Then, with a deep moan that seemed to come from his very soul, his lips moved against hers in hungry insistence as his arms encircled her and embraced her more tightly against him.

He stood up, pulling her up with him, and her body sought the contours of his, melding against his heat and strength. As she pressed intimately into him, she felt his desire for her, knew he could say whatever he wanted, but he couldn't deny the fact that his body hungered for hers. And as he tore his mouth away from hers, his eyes shone with a love that didn't lie.

He gazed at her, his expression infinitely gentle as his hand moved up and swept a strand of her hair away from her cheek. "Bonnie, if you won't leave here now...then promise me that when this little picnic Walter has planned is over, you'll leave then." His arms tightened around her, his hands caressing up and down her back, creating sensations that made it difficult for Bonnie to think rationally. "Promise me you won't let him make you stay any longer." His hands stopped moving and once again tightened around her. "Promise me you won't trust him."

Bonnie blinked rapidly in confusion. How could she deny this man anything? And yet how could she promise not to trust the man who had fathered her? She felt as if she was being torn in two...split between her need to understand Nicholas and her need to gain some sort of a relationship with her father. "I...don't... I can't..."

Nicholas released her slowly, reluctantly. "Just remember what I said," he whispered softly, casting a quick glance to the doorway, as if he feared someone listening to them. "Don't trust him." He raked a hand through his hair, and Bonnie felt his energy growing, filling the room. It was the strange electricity she'd noticed before that emanated off him in waves.

He walked toward the door that led onto the patio. "I need some air," he said, his voice thick, unusually deep.

He started out the door, turning back to look at her one last time, and his eyes glistened more silver than green. Then he was gone.

Bonnie moved over to the door and peered out into the night, where the moonlight cascaded down and painted the landscape in ghostlike fingers of light. A fine, vaporous mist enveloped the area, adding to the eerie atmosphere.

She saw Nicholas running toward the nearby tangled vegetation, his long, muscular legs carrying him gracefully across the length of the lawn.

When he reached the edge of the copse, he paused

in the shadows, looking back at where she stood. His eyes glowed across the space that separated them, although the shadows shrouded the shape of his body. Then, after a long moment, he turned and leapt into the brush, disappearing in the blink of her eye.

She stared after him, her heart thudding, pulsating so loudly in her temples she wondered if the rest of the people in the house could hear it. She placed her hand over her chest, telling herself to take a deep breath, her gaze not wavering from the place where Nicholas had disappeared.

I'm losing my mind, she thought, continuing to draw deep, cleansing breaths. It was the only explanation. It was a trick of her mind, an illusion produced by the fog. It was the strange moonlight or a figment of her imagination. There had to be a logical explanation.

Numbed, she walked on wooden legs back to the chair and dug into the cushions, pulling out the book she'd been reading before Nicholas had interrupted her.

She stared at it for a long moment, running a finger over the gold letters of the title. A shiver danced up her spine as she replayed in her mind what she thought she had just seen. In that single instant, when Nicholas had turned and leapt into the brush, she could have sworn he was covered in a thick, gray fur. She could have sworn he was a wolf.

* * *

There are no such things as werewolves. There are no such things as werewolves. The words played like a mantra in her mind the next morning.

Even though the midmorning sunshine streamed into the windows, Bonnie remained in bed, sitting up with the book about werewolves open on her lap. She studied the pictures, read and reread the text, and scoffed at it all. It was easier to scoff this morning in the light of day than it had been last night with the shadows of darkness surrounding her.

"Utterly ridiculous," she said aloud, slamming the book shut with a thud. "Oh, Mom, I'm really letting my imagination get away from me this time."

She kicked off the blankets and got out of bed.

"Werewolves, indeed," she muttered irritably as she dressed. Even if there were such things, it still wouldn't make any sense.

According to every legend she'd ever heard about the werewolf, the beast only came out on the night of a full moon. And there had yet to be a full moon since Bonnie had arrived at the Redding Institute. Of course, she could always shoot Nicholas with a silver bullet, and if he died, it would be proof that he was a werewolf. It would also be proof that he was merely human.

The whole thing was ridiculous…too ridiculous to even contemplate. Her mind went back to repeating the mantra. *There are no such things as werewolves, there are no such things as werewolves.*

* * *

By the time the morning of the promised picnic arrived, she had come to terms with the fact that whatever she thought she had seen that night in the fog, it had only been an illusion of her confused mind.

True to Walter's words, at noon they all piled into the red pickup truck. Bonnie was disappointed by Nicholas's absence. She'd hoped he would join them. She knew he was once again spending long hours down in the lab. What she hadn't realized until this moment was just how important he had become in her life. She awakened each morning anxious to see him and went to bed each night with him the last conscious thought before sleep claimed her. She held the memory of their lovemaking close to her heart, wanting to repeat the experience again and again. Man or beast...she loved him, and it frightened her to discover just how deep her love for him had become.

Jimmy drove the group about five miles from the house, where a huge pond sat at the edge of a large field that had recently been plowed over.

"Is this still part of the institute?" Bonnie asked curiously as she descended from the bed of the pickup.

Walter nodded. "Yes, but the land is farmed by people in Hollow Rock. It's a sort of rental arrangement with the town."

Bonnie looked over to where Mavis was unloading the baskets of food she had prepared. "Here, let me help with that." She hurried over to help, surprised when Mavis didn't object.

"Why don't we take everything over beneath those trees." Mavis pointed to where three large trees grouped together to form a large, shady area about a hundred yards from the pond's edge.

"Looks perfect," Bonnie agreed, picking up one of the large baskets and following Mavis. As they took care of the food, Walter and the other men got lawn chairs out of the back of the truck. "Hmm, something smells wonderful," Bonnie said when Mavis opened the lid of one of the baskets.

"Fried chicken," Mavis replied.

"That's one of my favorites," Bonnie answered.

Mavis grunted. "It was always one of your daddy's favorites, too."

Bonnie smiled, pleased finally to find something—anything—she had in common with her father. She grabbed the other end of the blanket Mavis had pulled out and helped her lay it down in the lush grass, smiling as her father and the other men joined them.

"Bonnie, my dear. Come and sit here next to me." Walter motioned toward a lawn chair. Pleased by his attention, she quickly complied, shoving thoughts of Nicholas out of her mind.

"Ah, it's a beautiful morning, isn't it?" Walter observed, looking every bit the powerful king surveying his kingdom.

"Gorgeous," Bonnie agreed, smiling as she

watched Jimmy tossing a Frisbee to the other scientists. It was obvious these were men accustomed to exercising their minds and not their bodies. As first one, then another, chased after the bright orange disc, Bonnie thought they looked like gangly teenagers, all arms and legs with no coordination or grace.

She tried to hide a smile as Dr. Wellsburn took a tumble, sprawling onto the grass in an unsuccessful attempt to catch the spinning Frisbee.

"This will probably be good for them," Walter said. "I've been working them very hard the past couple of months."

"Don't they have families?" Bonnie asked curiously, wondering about the men who shared the house with her father.

Walter shook his head. "These men were raised rather like hothouse flowers, in a controlled environment to maximize their intellectual potential."

"That sounds horrible," Bonnie replied, looking at the men once again.

"Perhaps, but they long ago accepted that their destinies reached far beyond that of ordinary men. Love, families, emotional entanglements—these are things these men don't need. They are destined for a much higher purpose."

Bonnie frowned. What could be a more noble cause than loving and being loved? What higher purpose could there be than making a commitment to another and together creating a new life? She started to say something, but seeing the fervent light in his eyes, she realized that she and her father would never share the same values. It was even difficult to believe that she shared a part of this man's genes.

Still, as the day wore on, she was grateful that she had decided to linger at the institute and give her father this last chance to connect with her.

Even though he didn't talk about Bonnie's mother, didn't touch on the brief years they'd shared together, he spoke at length about his life at the institute, sharing with her amusing stories of co-workers and townspeople, of power failures and computer glitches.

Bonnie drank it all in, her hunger to know him somewhat satiated by the little bits and pieces of himself he offered her.

Following lunch, the men sat on the blanket, their conversation, as always, reverting back to scientific formulas and problems far beyond Bonnie's grasp.

She touched Jimmy's shoulder and motioned for him to follow her to the edge of the pond. Once there, they sat down side by side. Bonnie grinned as Jimmy rolled up his pant legs and dipped his feet in the water, emitting a mock shiver to indicate that the water was cold. Something in his expression strummed the chord of an old memory in Bonnie's mind.

She frowned, wondering why on earth Jimmy's expression had pulled up a childish memory of her father. It was something in his smile, the way one corner of his mouth quirked upward crookedly.

Jimmy gazed at her quizzically and she smiled and quickly shook her head to let him know nothing was wrong. Whatever expression his face had momentarily contained that had reminded her of her father, was now gone, making her certain that she'd only imagined the similarity.

A dark shadow fell on both her and Jimmy, and they turned around to see Nicholas standing just behind where they sat.

"Nicholas!" Bonnie greeted him in pleased surprise. "I didn't think you were going to make it here today."

He sat down next to her, his strong thigh pressing intimately against hers, causing her heart to beat erratically against her rib cage. "I couldn't miss out on Mavis's fried chicken," he replied. "Besides, it isn't every day that the great Walter Redding calls a moratorium on his work." He turned and smiled at Jimmy. "Mavis is cutting the angel food cake."

Jimmy's eyes lit and he jumped up, causing both Nicholas and Bonnie to yelp in protest as he splashed them with the cold pond water. Still grinning, he grabbed his shoes and his socks and walked off toward the blanket where the others were enjoying Mavis's dessert.

Bonnie smiled warmly at Nicholas, knowing her heart was there in her eyes for him to see. He smiled back, and for just a brief moment the dark shadows lifted from his eyes and she saw the beauty of the man within shining through.

He broke the gaze, directing his attention toward the water, where the sunlight sparkled and danced on the surface. "You like your work as a teacher?" he asked suddenly.

"Oh yes, I can't imagine doing anything else. There's something very special about turning a child on to learning, seeing their eyes light up as they understand something new." She laughed apologetically. "Don't get me started—I'll bore you to death."

Nicholas smiled wistfully. "You could never bore me," he objected. "Besides, there was a time when I entertained thoughts of being a teacher, working with kids."

"Why didn't you?"

He shrugged. "Destiny had other plans for me."

Bonnie studied his face searchingly. Both he and her father had spoken of destiny, but as Bonnie thought of Nicholas growing old here at the institute, alone and isolated, she wondered if perhaps destiny hadn't made a horrible mistake.

She sensed that Nicholas was a man with an enormous wealth of love to give. But in this life-style he'd chosen, he would never have the opportunity to explore his own potential for love. And that was the biggest tragedy of all.

She turned to him, reaching out to take his hands in hers. "Nicholas...come with me when I leave here.

Come home with me. You can still be a teacher. We can leave here together first thing in the morning."

Raw pain tortured his features into a grimace and he tightened his grip on her hands, his eyes haunting her with their sadness, their obvious yearning for what she offered. "I can't." His answer was a tormented whisper. "I can't leave here."

"Why not?" Bonnie asked, her heart breaking at his anguish.

He took a deep breath and released it with a shudder. "I told you that I'd sold my soul, and nothing has changed."

"You work here," Bonnie protested. "Nobody owns your soul. It's a job, Nicholas, and men quit jobs all the time." She broke off in frustration as he shook his head, denying the validity of her words. "Nicholas, that night after we made love, you asked me what I wanted from you, and I said nothing." Bonnie's voice trembled with emotion, and she realized this would be her last plea to him. She knew he cared for her, it was in his eyes, transmitted in the touch of his hand holding hers. But something held his love captive, and she knew she couldn't fight what she didn't understand. "I lied when I told you I didn't want anything from you. I do want something from you...I want your love."

He closed his eyes, his grip on her hands almost painful. "Dear God, Bonnie. You're killing me." He opened his eyes and gazed at her, emitting the strange, silvery hue that she now realized always preceded his anger. "You're killing me with your dreams...with your love." He jerked his hands out of hers and stood up. He seemed to grow, somehow looking larger as he loomed over her, his eyes flashing their metallic intensity. "Bonnie, please...take your dreams and go home."

Without waiting for her reply, he took off running, his long legs carrying him swiftly toward the dense cover of the nearby woods. "Nicholas...wait," she called after him.

"My dear, you seem to have quite an unusual effect on Nicholas." Walter spoke from just behind her, his deep voice an unwanted intrusion.

Bonnie stood up to face her father, who stared after Nicholas, a thoughtful expression on his face. "What on earth did you say to him?" he asked, looking at her curiously.

"It doesn't matter," she replied hollowly, her heart aching.

"Well, my dear. It's time to load up the truck and go back to the house. It's early enough we should still be able to get a little work done tonight." He took her arm and patted it gently, but his touch did nothing to chase away the pain in Bonnie's heart.

She realized at that moment that in the past couple of days she had finally outgrown the need for her father. She was no longer a little girl. It was too late to recapture that which was lost to time and circumstance.

She was now a woman, and her need was for the man who had disappeared into the forest…the man whose tortured soul cried out to her.

CHAPTER TEN

"**Y**es, come in," Bonnie called, sitting up in her bed at the knock on her door. She felt a twinge of disappointment as her father walked in. She had hoped...

"My dear, Mavis tells me you're planning on leaving first thing in the morning. I so enjoyed the picnic today, but we've scarcely gotten to know one another."

And whose fault was that? Bonnie wanted to say, but didn't. What was the point? "I enjoyed today, too, but it's time to leave. I do have a life to get back to."

Walter crossed the room and perched on the side of her bed. "Stay a bit longer. We still have so much to discover about each other. Besides, I worry about you going back home. It's much too soon following your mother's death." His expression was one of fatherly concern, but Bonnie viewed him objectively, realizing it was a case of too little, too late. There was nothing here for her. Nothing at all. The man her mother had told her about, the warm, loving man she'd always imagined as her father, didn't exist, perhaps had never existed except in her mother's lovestruck mind.

"I appreciate your concern, but I'll be just fine,"

she exclaimed, suddenly unable to wait until morning to get away from this place. She was exhausted, disappointed at having to put away her childish dreams of her father, emotionally broken apart by thoughts of leaving Nicholas.

"Are you sure I can't change your mind and talk you into staying a bit longer?" Walter pressed.

"Positive," Bonnie replied firmly. "I'm already packed." She gestured to her suitcase sitting by the bedroom door. "It's time I go back home."

"Well, my dear, then I guess we'll save our actual goodbyes for the morning." He stood up as a soft knock fell on her door. "Ah, that will be Mavis. I had her fix you something extraspecial." He opened the door and took the cup and saucer from Mavis, then turned back to Bonnie. "As far as I'm concerned, there's nothing better than a nice hot cup of cocoa after a long day." He set the drink on her bedside stand, then, with a gentle smile and a good-night, he turned and left her room.

Bonnie stared at the cup of steaming dark brew, an alien cold beginning in the pit of her stomach and quickly sweeping throughout her. Cocoa…he had brought her cocoa.

Her heart thudded in her chest as she stared at the drink, other remembered incidents feeding her growing anxiety. The apple fritters sent by Lauretta…her father's favorite doughnuts, but not eaten by the man calling himself Walter Redding. His lack of memories concerning Bonnie's mother, his dog, Bonnie herself.

She'd felt the strange tension from the moment she'd arrived at the institute, but now it seemed insidious, evil...and infinitely more dangerous. She suddenly realized that there was no way in hell that the man calling himself Walter Redding was her father. And if that man wasn't her father...then what had happened to the real Walter Redding?

"Maybe I'm wrong," she whispered aloud, placing her hand over her chest in an effort to still the rapid beating of her heart.

Perhaps he'd just forgotten she was deathly allergic to chocolate. He'd certainly forgotten a million other things, as well. He'd apologized for his poor memory. She clung to this thought desperately, but she just didn't believe it. How could he have forgotten?

One of her strongest memories of her father was of the night she'd spent in the hospital after a near-fatal allergic reaction to a candy bar. She could still remember the feel of her father's hands as he'd tenderly stroked her forehead. She could remember his deep voice, easing her fears as she fought for each labored breath. She could remember him teasing her, telling her she would never be able to enjoy the pleasure of a box of chocolates brought to her by a special beau.

How could he forget something so monumental in her life? How could he forget so easily what had been one of the major traumas of her childhood? He hadn't forgotten...he had never known. Once again, cold arctic winds of horror swept over her, through her.

Who was this man who had taken her father's name and stepped into his life? And where was her real father? Where was the real Walter Redding? What had happened to him?

She got out of bed and pulled on a pair of jeans and a sweatshirt. She needed to find some answers. She paused a moment, confusion furrowing her brows. Who could she ask? Who could she trust?

Nicholas? His name exploded in her head, causing her to reel in shock. What part did he have in this masquerade? Did he know that the man he worked for was not the real Walter Redding? Suddenly everything he had ever said to her replayed in her mind, taking on new dimensions, frightening dimensions. She needed to talk to Nicholas, immediately. She needed to know what the hell was going on.

After gazing out into the darkened hallway and seeing nobody around, she tiptoed down the hall toward Nicholas's rooms. Once there, she knocked softly on the door, listening intently for movement within. Not a sound escaped through the thick door.

Once again Bonnie knocked, this time harder, in desperation. Still there was no reply. Nicholas wasn't there.

She hurried back to her room, her mind whirling as she tried to figure out what to do next. She was frightened, but she was also determined to discover the truth. But how? Where could she go, who could she ask? She no longer knew who she could trust.

She suddenly thought about the room in the lab…the private one she hadn't been invited in to see, the one that was Walter Redding's personal office. Perhaps she would find some answers there.

Looking once again at the clock next to her bed, she realized it was far too early to venture downstairs to the lab. She needed to wait until everyone else in the house was asleep. She eased herself down in the chair by the fireplace, staring into the flames.

She wrapped her arms around herself, trying to ward off the chill that froze her from within. She sat and waited for the night to deepen, waited for the house to sleep.

It was nearly two in the morning when Bonnie finally crept down the stairway to the laboratory, a flashlight clutched painfully tight in her hand, illuminating her way through the unfamiliar territory.

She touched the doorknob of the private office, sending a small prayer upward. If it was locked, she didn't know what she would do. She knew instinctively that if she was going to find answers, it would be here, in this room.

Twisting the doorknob, feeling it turn easily beneath her touch, she released a sigh of relief. She should have known it wouldn't be locked. The man calling himself Walter Redding was arrogant, secure in his godlike control over the others. He wouldn't dream that anyone would dare enter his private sanctuary.

Shining the flashlight around the small room, she was surprised at the lack of equipment, the very barrenness of the room. Other than a large desk, a file cabinet and a computer, the room was empty.

She paused, unsure where to begin as she realized she didn't know exactly what she was looking for. Tentatively, she sat down at the computer and pressed the power button. Although she wasn't an electronics whiz, she did know how to read files. Perhaps she would find some answers to her questions in the memory of the machine.

She was relieved to find the computer user-friendly and was easily able to locate a directory of file names. Scanning down the list, her heart jumped as she saw a file labeled *Bonnie*.

With trembling fingers, she pulled up the file and began to read.

My dearest Bonnie:
It is now, when I realize there is little time left for me, that I look back and regret decisions made a lifetime ago.

I am ill, and have been ill for quite some time now. My work has become unimportant as I realize that in the great scheme of things, I achieved my greatest accomplishment when you were conceived. I only regret that I was not there to watch you grow, to share your joys and ease your heartaches.

Bonnie continued reading, the words blurring as tears misted her vision. She swiped at her eyes, finding in her father's words the love she'd needed. The letter told her of his decision to come to the institute, of his attempt to get her mother to join him here. He spoke of the difficulty in maintaining their long-distance relationship, the quiet companionship he'd discovered with Mavis, his feelings of guilt and his undying love for his first-born child, Bonnie.

The letter ended abruptly on the fifth page. At the very end were a bunch of symbols and letters Bonnie didn't understand. She scanned the remaining list of files, seeing nothing of interest, then shut off the computer, still as confused as ever.

Although she still had no proof, she knew in her heart that the letter had not been written by the man who had brought her the hot cocoa. That man, with his cold blue eyes and chilling disinterest, couldn't be the man who'd written the emotional letter she'd just finished reading.

She opened the desk drawers, rummaging through papers and office supplies, but found nothing of interest in any of them. She then went to the metal file cabinet and began going through the manila folders, unsure what exactly she hoped to find, but instinctively knowing she would recognize it when she saw it.

It was at the back of the file cabinet that she found her proof—photos…the missing photos from the album. As she picked them up, her hands began trembling once again, the shock of betrayal, the horror of knowledge racing through her. The pictures were of her mother and her father…wedding-day photos, honeymoon pictures…photos of Bonnie and her dad, her dad with Jackemo.

Although the pictures were old, showing a much younger man, Bonnie saw why they had been removed. They were positive proof that the man calling himself Walter Redding was not the real Walter Redding.

She stared at them hungrily, taking in each feature, every minute detail of her father's face. And in him, she saw her own firm jawline, her vivid green eyes, and she cried.

The tears were painful, oozing out from beneath her eyelids as she stifled her sobs, afraid that any noise might travel upstairs and alert somebody to her presence here.

Tears finally spent, she rubbed at her eyes and picked up the last of the photos on her lap. This one was more recent, showing her father and the man who'd been living her father's life standing at the front door of the institute. She turned the photo over. Walter Redding and Jonathon Dennison. The names were written on the back, and she stared at them in horror, for a moment refusing to believe the implication.

If the man calling himself Walter Redding was really Jonathon Dennison...then who was buried out in the grave in the backyard?

"No." The denial tore from her throat, creating a sharp, vivid pain deep in her chest. She stumbled from the office and up the stairs, blinded by the hot tears that once again coursed down her cheeks.

She stifled a scream as she walked right into a big, broad chest. She looked up in horror, afraid of who she'd bumped into. Her flashlight played on him, his eyes wild and untamed in the beam of light. "Nicholas," she sobbed in relief, and without thinking she went into his arms, needing somebody to help ease the deep grief that tore at her insides.

"Bonnie...what's the matter?" Nicholas's arms tightened around her, pulling her against his warmth. "What's going on?"

"My...my father...he's...he's dead." Sobs choked in her chest as she tightened her grip on Nicholas, needing his strength to steady her wobbly legs.

"Shhh," he cautioned her, glancing around worriedly. "Come on, we need to talk." Wordlessly he led her up the stairs, past her room and to his, where he opened the door and took her over to the bed. Once there, he cradled her like a child, rocking her and stroking her hair as she gave in to deep sobs that racked her body.

Time passed, a lifetime for Bonnie as she shed tears for the father she had loved, the man she would now never know. Her grief was doubled with the knowledge that she was now totally alone in the world. No, not totally alone.

As Nicholas soothed her, surrounded her with his strength, she felt her grief ebbing, being replaced by a need so great it threatened to consume her.

She raised her head and gazed at the man she had come to love with all her heart, all her soul. In the semidarkness of the room, with only the light from the fire, she saw his eyes answer hers, flaming to life with a desire to match her own. With a small groan he covered her mouth with his, filling her with a heat that eased the cold knot of grief in her heart.

She drank of him, loving the hot wildness of his mouth. The scent of him heightened her desire. He smelled of the outdoors, as if he'd been running in the moonlight, embracing the wind. And she wanted the wildness of his lovemaking to take her away from her grief, consume her into a vortex so black it contained no room for thought.

She lay back on the bed, beckoning him to join her there. "Make love to me, Nicholas. Please." She opened her arms to him as, with a groan of acquiescence, he moved over her, his mouth once again hot and insistent against hers.

As his lips worked their magic, his hands reached up beneath her sweatshirt, capturing her unbound breasts eagerly. In one graceful movement he rolled over, moving to his back with her on top straddling him. As he pulled up the bottom of her sweatshirt, she raised her hands above her, allowing him to sweep the shirt over her head and to the floor.

Her fingers trembled as she unbuttoned his shirt, wanting to feel the erotic roughness of his chest hair against her soft breasts. Once the shirt was removed, she leaned forward, allowing his mouth access to her already turgid nipples. He kissed one, then the other, his tongue lathing the sensitive tips until she thought she'd lose her mind.

She moved to the side of him, her fingers working the zipper of his jeans, feeling his desire taut against the denim material. His eyes were silver orbs glowing brilliantly in the dimly lit room as he helped her with the task, kicking off his pants. The illumination from the fire painted his body in a reddish gold hue that emphasized the strength of his muscles, the beauty of his nakedness.

Bonnie moved away from him, standing at the side of the bed to remove her own jeans. As she slid her silk panties down her legs, she saw the effect she had on him, watching in awe as his desire grew and the light in his eyes intensified.

She moved back onto the bed and their bodies sought the contours of each other. Bonnie gave herself to him, body and soul, and he took her, loving each hollow, caressing every part of her. He loved her inside and out, his hands and mouth touching her body while his soul entwined with hers.

Bonnie returned his caresses, enamored by the feel of him, the taste of him. And when they were both panting, beyond thought, beyond sanity, he entered her.

He filled her up completely, and as he began to move within her, she clutched at his shoulders, matching her rhythm to his. His mouth covered hers, his tongue moving inside as his body thrust deeper into her.

He withdrew his mouth, his rhythm increasing, and Bonnie opened her eyes, drowning in the depths of his, losing sight of the world around her. For a long moment, he became her world, obliterating everything else in the room, everything else in her life. With a cry, she gave herself to the shattering of senses, allowing pure sensation to carry her over the edge and into a climax so intense it left her gasping his name over and over again.

Still he continued, thrusting deep and strong, swiftly taking her once again to the pinnacle of pleasure, this time tumbling with her into a thunderous explosion of reality.

Afterward they lay together unmoving, Bonnie's head resting on his chest, his heartbeat echoing the strong, steady rhythm of her own. Gently, the fingers of one hand tangled in the hair of his chest, caressing the smooth, muscled skin beneath. ''You knew, didn't you?'' she said softly, not looking at him. ''You knew that my father was dead, that Walter was really Jonathon Dennison.''

There was a long pause, and when he answered, his voice was filled with a singular sadness. ''Yes, I knew.''

Bonnie squeezed her eyes tightly closed, a sob once again choking in her chest. She'd hoped that he would tell her she was wrong, that no matter what photos she'd found, no matter what information she'd gained, her dad wasn't dead and buried in the backyard. But his answer banished the last lingering remnant of hope. She raised herself up on her elbows and gazed at him. ''Why? Why didn't you tell me?'' she asked, a note of angry betrayal in her voice.

''I couldn't.'' He rolled out of bed and pulled on his jeans, his features stark in the glow of the dying fire. ''Bonnie, Jonathon swore he would kill you if I told you the truth. And God help us, the man is crazy enough to do it.''

''Did he do something to my dad? Did he kill him?'' She clutched the blankets tightly around her, colder than she had ever been in her life.

Nicholas raked a hand through his hair. ''No...I don't know,'' he confessed. ''Your father was sick. I'm not even sure what was wrong with him. All I know is that each day he got weaker and weaker, and every day Jonathon took over more and more control. One morning we found Walter dead. He died in his sleep, but I don't know if Jonathon had something to do with his death or not.''

''But what about the death certificate—isn't there some sort of law demanding an autopsy to determine the cause of death?''

Nicholas smiled grimly. ''Here at the institute, Jonathon is the law. There was no death certificate, because he didn't want anyone to know that Walter was dead.''

Bonnie sat up and stared at him. ''But why? Why is he pretending to be my father? What possible reason can he have for this charade?''

''Funding.'' Nicholas crossed to the bed and sat down next to her. ''Your father was a brilliant man, Bonnie. The pharmaceutical company who set up the institute, the people who hired him, gave him unlimited funds, they bought Walter Redding's brilliance. Without that, the funding would stop.''

''You mean to tell me, all this is about money?'' She stared at him incredulously.

''And power.''

''But after my father's death, why couldn't Jonathon just go out and get his own funding? He's obviously a brilliant man.''

Nicholas nodded. ''Yes, Jonathon is brilliant, perhaps even more so than your father. Unfortunately, in the scientific community, Jonathon had developed a reputation for being something of a renegade. He didn't follow rules, he stepped over the morality lines. Nobody would have given him money for research. Nobody trusted him.''

Bonnie frowned, grappling with everything she'd been told. "Then why would my father hire such a man?''

"Walter recognized Jonathon's brilliance, and I think he truly thought he could control him, keep him in check.'' He reached out and gathered her back in his arms. "I'm sorry, Bonnie. I wanted to tell you everything. I wanted you to leave here before you learned of your father's death. I wanted you to go before Jonathon tainted whatever good memories you had of your father.'' He once again stroked her hair as she leaned her head against his chest.

She closed her eyes, allowing his gentle touch to soothe her. There was a certain amount of relief in the thought that the cold, distant scientist wasn't her father. But that relief mingled with a deep sadness that she would never know the man her mother had loved, the one who had written her the beautiful note. "Did you know him?'' she asked.

"Your father was the reason I came here. It wasn't only his exceptional mind that attracted me. It was his warmth and humor that made me decide to work for him. He was a good man, Bonnie. He had dreams of making the world a better place with his DNA and genetic research.''

As if Nicholas sensed her need to know more, he settled back on the bed and continued. "He spoke of you and your mother often. From what he told me, your mother refused to be stuck away in the backwoods of Arkansas and he couldn't do his work anywhere but here."

Bonnie slowly digested this information. It had never before entered her mind that perhaps her parents' separation had been as much her mother's choice as her father's. "What about Mavis?" she asked suddenly. "What kind of relationship did she have with my father?"

"I'm not really sure. It was complicated. I know at one time years ago they had an intimate one, but I think in the last couple of years it was more a deep friendship than anything else."

Bonnie nodded, surprised to find a certain satisfaction in the knowledge that her father had had Mavis to ease the loneliness of this place. She thought again of Jimmy, the grief that had etched deeply in his face on the day they had stood at the grave in the yard. If the man buried there was Jimmy's father... "Then Jimmy is my half brother," Bonnie said aloud, suddenly realizing why at the pond that day she'd seen a vague similarity to her father. Rather than bringing her fresh pain, the thought of Jimmy brought a small smile to her lips. A brother...a piece of a family she never knew she had. How could she be sorry to discover that the freckle-faced boy with the gentle smile and love of flowers was her half brother?

She sat up suddenly, pushing a strand of her hair off her face. "We have to do something." She eased herself out of Nicholas's arms and off the bed. "We have to go to the authorities," she said, yanking on her jeans and reaching for her sweatshirt. She quickly pulled it over her head, then stepped into her shoes and turned back to him. "I'm not waiting another minute longer. Jonathon Dennison belongs in jail." She reached out and grabbed his hands. "Come on, Nicholas. Together we'll go to the sheriff, and you'll be free of this place and that man forever."

Nicholas shook his head and removed his hands from hers. "I can't leave here. I told you that before. There is still something you don't know."

Bonnie looked at him, a sense of dread suddenly sweeping over her. What could possibly be worse than what she had just heard? What else could he possibly have to tell her? "What?" she finally asked, her voice a whisper of dread.

He stared into the fire, his features taut with tension. "Bonnie, it's me. I'm not what you think I am."

"Nicholas." She reached for his hands once again, holding tightly as he attempted to pull them away. "The time for secrets is over. Tell me what I don't know…tell me what it is about you that's eating you up inside."

He looked at her, his mouth working soundlessly

as if trying to find the right words. "Bonnie, I...I've been part of an experiment. My body has been altered."

She studied him with confusion. "I don't understand." She'd made love to him, caressed each and every part of his body. There was nothing altered about him.

"It's not on the outside," he explained. "It's on the inside. My DNA has been changed."

Bonnie's heart seemed to skip a beat. "What do you mean? Are you ill? I don't understand." She squeezed his hands desperately, afraid of what he was saying, afraid because she didn't—couldn't—understand. "Tell me, Nicholas. For God's sake, tell me."

Once again he jerked his hands out of hers, rising from the bed and stalking to the window. He stood for a long moment, his back to her. His silence filled the room more loudly than anything Bonnie had ever heard. She held her breath. "It's not an illness," he finally said. "At least, not in the traditional sense."

She stared at him in irritated disbelief. "My God, Nicholas. I've just learned that my father is dead, possibly murdered. What could be worse than that?"

He turned around and looked at her, then smiled, a strange smile that made Bonnie's stomach clench in dread. A log fell in the grate, shooting sparks that danced against the glass doors of the fireplace and momentarily filled the room with glowing light.

But Nicholas's face was dark...dark with a mystery Bonnie suddenly didn't want to know.

His smile appeared almost feral in the fire's glow, and his eyes radiated with the strange, silver hue. "What could possibly be worse? Bonnie, I'm a were-wolf."

CHAPTER ELEVEN

For a moment his words hung in the air, seeming to suck out all the oxygen, making it difficult for Bonnie to breathe. She stared at him, willing him to laugh, to tell her it was all a crazy joke. "Right, and I'm the tooth fairy," she retorted uneasily.

"Bonnie, this is real." His eyes bore into her, and again she felt a breathless kind of fear. "I am a werewolf."

"But that's impossible." She heard the nervous laughter in her voice, but she had no control over it. "That's just a legend, a crazy myth. There's no such thing, and I don't believe you." It was absolutely impossible. What he'd said had no place in the real world, in her world. She looked around, seeing a normal bedroom, finding comfort in the mundane brown cord bedspread and cotton sheets. This was a man's room...not a monster's.

"Nicholas, if this is some ploy so you don't have to make a commitment to me, it isn't necessa—" She swallowed the last of the sentence on a gasp as he stalked across the room and gripped her shoulders tightly.

"Don't do that."

"Don't do what?" she whispered, smelling his wildness, captivated by the fierce intensity of his eyes.

"Don't turn this into some silly man-woman game. This is my life…this is my torment, to love you and know I'll never have you." His hands caressed her shoulders through the material of her sweatshirt. Anguish filled his face as he gazed deep into her eyes. "I take your image with me when I lose my sanity, slip out of consciousness and become a nightmare creature capable of evil."

"You could never be capable of evil. Evil isn't in you."

"Dammit, Bonnie!" He released his grip on her shoulders and instead covered his face. His body trembled with the force of his emotions and he drew deep breaths as if to steady himself. When he withdrew his hands from his face, his features were expressionless, his eyes a dull, empty green.

"Those animals Jimmy found in the forest, the ones that had been mutilated and torn apart…they were the work of a beast. My work, Bonnie…only mine."

"That's impossible," she whispered, her legs losing their strength as she felt reality shift and fall away, plunging her into a nightmare world.

He grabbed her hand and pulled her across the floor to the other side of the room and opened a door. "Look inside, Bonnie. This is where I try to come when I feel a transformation beginning."

With dreadful hesitation, Bonnie looked into the room, her nostrils flaring as she breathed in the wild, gamy scent of the room. It was a room from an insane asylum...a padded room without furniture, without windows.

Maybe he was crazy. She grasped on to the idea hopefully. Perhaps he only *thought* he turned into a werewolf. Lycanthropy...wasn't that the term for the disease that made people believe they were werewolves? Yes, of course, that was it. He suffered a strange dementia that made him believe he turned into a werewolf.

Yet, even as she clung to this thought, doubt tickled at her insides with cold fingers. The air in the padded cell smelled thick, potent with animal scent...and she wondered if perhaps she was the one who was insane and this whole thing was a figment of her overstressed, overworked imagination.

"It's real, Bonnie," he said as if reading her thoughts. "I wish to God it wasn't, but it is." He led her back across the room to a door on the opposite wall. Jaw muscles taut, he opened this door and stepped back, allowing her to look inside.

She peered in and gasped in shock. The room had once been another bedroom, but it now lay in ruins. The mattress on the bed had been ripped to shreds, exposing the twisted bedsprings beneath. The heavy curtains were shredded, as if sharpened steel spikes had raked down them, leaving behind only tattered cloth. What had once been a chair, now lay in a pile of splintered, useless hardwood. Total destruction... unbelievable devastation...

It looked as if a wild, angry animal had been caged inside. *This isn't proof that he's a werewolf,* she told herself. *He could have done this in some sort of insane fit.*

"I was staying in this room the first time I transformed. I've kept it in this condition to remind myself of what I am...what I'm capable of becoming."

Bonnie nodded numbly, closing the door to shut out the sight of the destroyed room. On wobbly legs, she walked back over to the bed and sat down on the edge of the mattress, her mind unable to comprehend all she'd just learned. "You left the book for me to find," she said softly. "The book about werewolves."

He nodded. "I wanted to tell you, but I was afraid of what Jonathon would do. I hoped you'd read the book, know there was something horrible here, and leave."

"I...I don't understand. How is this possible? How did this happen to you?" She still didn't quite believe. How could she? And yet... She looked at him searchingly, her mind seeking sanity, concrete answers that made sense. "Is it safe to assume that you weren't bitten by a wolf?" Even to her own ears, the question sounded utterly ridiculous. Her mind raced through all that she had read in the book, trying to relate all she knew of werewolves to the man standing before her.

"I was not bitten by a wolf and I don't bay at full moons," he agreed with a touch of wryness.

He moved back over to stand before the window, turning his back to her and looking out into the night darkness. The fire hissed and spat, the golden glow painting his naked back in stark relief, emphasizing the strength and symmetry. "I had been here a couple months when I developed a bad cold. It was really no big deal, just irritating. A scratchy throat, a cough that kept me from sleeping...the usual cold symptoms. Anyway, Jonathon came in here one night and told me he thought an injection of vitamins would help me kick it."

He turned away from the window and faced Bonnie. "I trusted him. I bared my arm and he gave me the injection." His face darkened visibly and the glow of his eyes intensified. "For three days I stayed in bed, praying for death. My body burned up, the pain was excruciating and I was half-delirious." He smiled tightly. "Needless to say, it wasn't a shot of vitamins Jonathon gave me. It was an injection of a DNA modifier your father had been working on. Your father had tried it on a monkey and had been surprised at the unexpected negative results. Jonathon took the basic formula and made some adjustments. The shot he gave me bonded my DNA with that of a wolf's. By this time, your father was quite ill and Jonathon had pretty well taken over control of everything. When Walter learned what Jonathon had done to me, they had a terrible fight. By morning, Walter was dead.''

For a long moment Bonnie looked at him, appalled by what had been done to him in the name of science by a man who obviously had no concern for humanity. She still didn't know what to believe. What he had just told her was far too horrid to believe. ''Is there no cure?''

''I've been working on a formula to reverse the effects, but so far no luck. I don't even know the full effects of the drug.'' His eyes were bleak, hopeless. ''When I first realized what had been done to me, I was devastated, so afraid that I would harm somebody. As a scientist, I considered all the options, even taking my own life, but I realized my first priority had to be to find a cure and stop Jonathon. He can't do this to anyone else.'' He released a shuddering sigh, then continued. ''My biggest fear is that one time I'll transform and I'll remain a wolf forever. I won't be able to find my way back to my humanness.'' In three long strides he moved to stand before her. Kneeling down, he took her hands in his. ''Bonnie, you must leave here. Don't go to the authorities, don't let Jonathon know what you know. Just leave here and go back to your life.''

''I can't do that. I can't just walk away from all this,'' Bonnie protested. She looked down at his hands holding hers. He had strong hands, hands that had soothed her, stroked her, caressed her to a mind-lessness she'd never before known. Yet, to believe those same hands turned into paws, with nails that could shred curtains, crush bones…it was simply too much to handle. "Jonathon has to pay for what he's done. I have to tell somebody."

"Bonnie, if you tell someone, they'll come here and close down the laboratory. They'll lock me up in another lab and study me, analyze me. At least as long as I'm here, I can continue to work on an antidote. But if they lock me away somewhere, I'll never be free."

"Then I'll stay here. I'll wait for you to find the cure, then together we'll go to the authorities."

"Don't you understand? I love you," he exploded, rising up from the floor and stalking over to the window once again. He closed his eyes and took several deep breaths, then looked at her once again. "But every minute that you're near me, you're in danger. Every second that you remain here, your life is in jeopardy. I have very little control over the beast inside me. It feeds on my anger, and more and more of the time I can't control the anger raging inside me. My very soul would die if I hurt you. Bonnie, for the love of God, if you care about me, if you care about my sanity, my soul, you'll leave here."

Bonnie gazed at him, seeing his torture, feeling his torment. She didn't know what the truth was, but she couldn't help but hurt with his obvious anguish. She stood up and walked over to him, wrapping her arms around him and burying her head in his chest. Tears spilled from her eyes as she felt him hesitate, then he enfolded her close. "Please leave," he whispered raggedly, his pain raw and bleeding in his voice.

Through the mist of her tears, she looked up at him, looking through the depths of his eyes into the creature within. She saw not a monster, not a beast…she saw only the man she loved with all her heart and she knew she would leave because of her love. She wouldn't go for her own physical safety, but she would leave to guard the safety of his soul.

He saw her assent in her eyes, and he sagged against her in relief. For a long moment, they merely held each other, Bonnie listening to the beat of his heart beneath her ear. Too soon, his lips found her temple, then he gently shoved her away. "Go first thing in the morning. Give Jonathon the acting performance of your life. Don't let him know that you suspect anything's amiss." He reached out and gently swept a strand of her hair away from her forehead. "Bonnie…I love you." He dropped his hands from her shoulders and turned away from her. "Go now," he said abruptly.

"Nicholas, I—"

"Bonnie, for the love of God, get out of here. I'm out of control and I don't want you to see me."

Bonnie backed out of the room, feeling the enormous growing energy that surged in the air around him. For just a moment she lingered in the doorway, needing one last look, knowing instinctively that it would have to last her a lifetime.

His back was still to her, but he seemed to grow in proportion. With a growing sense of horror, Bonnie saw the muscles in his back shifting and moving beneath the skin…moving and shifting in a fashion that was distinctly abnormal. He raised his hands and gripped his head, stumbling down on one knee. Bonnie took a step toward him, his pain crying to her, killing her. "Go!" he thundered, his voice raspy and unnaturally deep.

Bonnie suddenly knew everything he'd told her was true. He was a werewolf. She paused only a moment longer, tears blurring her vision, then she turned and ran down the darkened hallway.

Nicholas slowly dragged himself toward the padded room, the pain in his head and body making conscious thought nearly impossible. *Bonnie…* His heart cried as he closed the door behind him and carefully secured it, locking himself in. *Bonnie…* His soul screamed as he curled up on the floor, the searing heat coursing through him causing him to reach for the oblivion of unconsciousness. The last thing he remembered before he gave in to the soothing blackness was yelling her name and hearing the echo of a savage, hoarse growl.

Bonnie stood in the middle of her bedroom, tears running down her face like raindrops on a windowpane. *Nicholas*... Her heart cried in anguish. Oh God, how could this be happening?

She swiped at her face and wrapped her arms around herself. She was cold...colder than she'd ever been. Her father's death was a tragedy, but what had been done to Nicholas had been criminal, a sin against nature and God. His torment twisted in her soul, his pain rippled in her heart.

A werewolf... Even after seeing the evidence, recognizing the truth, it was all still so difficult to believe. She shivered as she remembered the destruction of the room, thought of the dead animals that had been ripped apart. Her heart rebelled at the thought that Nicholas could be a part of that, but her head recognized the truth.

The curse of the beast is to kill those he most loves. The words from the book replayed in her mind. Although Nicholas wasn't a werewolf in the true sense of the word, it seemed that particular legend was what he feared most. He was afraid for her.

She remembered that moment when she'd confronted the wolf in the woods, thinking of that momentary instant when she'd felt a peculiar connection with the creature. Was it the part of the beast that still retained the essence of Nicholas that had somehow called to her? Even then, had she known someplace deep in her soul that Nicholas and the wolf were one and the same?

How on earth could she go downstairs in the morning, see Jonathon Dennison and pretend she didn't know that he was the real monster of the Redding Institute? How could she pretend everything was fine when her whole world had been tilted askew?

But you have to do just that, a small voice whispered inside her. She had to pretend for Nicholas's sake. She had to pretend and walk away, forget about Nicholas and everything that had happened here. It was impossible. She could fool Jonathon and leave the Redding Institute, but she could never, ever forget Nicholas.

She opened the French doors and stepped out onto the balcony. The darkness of the night embraced her with chilly arms, but the chill found a home in her heart, which she knew would never be warm again.

Someplace out there in the darkness was her father's grave. He'd died alone, been buried unmourned. But that's not quite true, she reminded herself, remembering Jimmy's grief-filled eyes as he'd pulled the weeds around the gravestone. At least her father had had Jimmy and Mavis. "And he did love me," she whispered to the moon, thinking of the letter she'd found in the computer in the laboratory.

She wanted a copy of that letter. The desire struck her suddenly. The letter was the only tangible proof she had of her father's love for her, and she couldn't stand the thought of leaving this godforsaken place without a copy.

She knew that if she was going to get a printout, it would have to be right now while the rest of the household slept. She paused at her doorway, gazing down the darkened hallway toward Nicholas's rooms, then down the other way. Nobody stirred, not a sound broke the stillness of the night.

For the second time, she snuck down the stairs toward the lab, not breathing until she was back in the private room, the computer humming to life.

She had just pulled up the directory of files when the door creaked open and the light overhead flipped on. She looked up with a gasp to see Jonathon Dennison standing in the doorway.

"My dear, what on earth are you doing?" His tone was light, but his eyes were radiant blue chunks of ice.

"Oh…uh…Father." The word tasted foul on Bonnie's lips, but she knew her life depended on what she was about to say. "I…I couldn't sleep and I was wandering around." She forced a small burst of laughter. "I confess, I was intrigued by the lab and the work you've been doing down here." She reached out and pushed the power button on the computer. "I'm sorry, Father, I should have asked your permission."

Jonathon's lips curved upward into a smile and he clapped his hands as if in applause. "Bravo, Bonnie, a wonderful performance, but not quite good enough."

"Wha—what do you mean?" Her heart began a rapid tattoo in her chest.

"I guess you and Nicholas didn't realize how your voices carry. Such a touching scene."

"You were spying on us," Bonnie accused, realizing her act was pointless. She suddenly remembered the other times she'd felt somebody watching her.

"Not spying…observing," he corrected. He shook his head, clucked his tongue and gazed at her with pity. "Really, my dear, it would have been so much easier had you simply drank the cocoa I brought to you. By the time you would have awakened, the injection would have been given."

"Injection?" Bonnie's blood ran cold. Fear overwhelmed her, tasting foul in her mouth, making the room seem to tilt and spin. "What are you talking about?" she asked, although she knew…dear God, she knew.

Jonathon leaned against the doorjamb, as relaxed as if he were discussing the weather with a group of intimate friends. "I allowed you to come here because I thought it would be interesting to observe the effects of an attractive female on Nicholas." The blue of his eyes intensified, and another bloodless smile played on his mouth. "And indeed, it has been fascinating. But now, the experiment continues."

"Continues how?" Bonnie wanted to run, but there was no place to go, no way to get past Jonathon.

"Once you are injected and experiencing transformations, it won't be long before you and Nicholas find each other and mate.'' His pupils dilated with pleasure at the thought, and Bonnie recognized that the man standing before her was completely insane. ''And your whelp will be the first of its kind, the parent to a new race of people.''

''And what if we don't? What if Nicholas and I don't…mate?'' she asked, stalling for time, her mind desperately seeking a means of escape.

He looked at her in confusion, as if the idea had never occurred to him. ''Oh, but you will,'' he said with undeniable certainty. ''There's already an elemental lust between the two of you. Once you both assume wolf form, that lust will explode, and believe me, you'll follow the natural instinct and you'll mate.''

Nicholas, Bonnie's heart cried, but she knew he couldn't help her. She thought of the moment before she had run out of his room, when his voice had deepened and she'd known he'd begun a transformation. ''You can't be serious,'' she exclaimed to Jonathon.

''Oh, my dear. I'm dead serious.'' The gun he pulled out of his pocket spoke more eloquently than any words. ''Now, if you'll be so kind as to come into the lab area.'' He motioned for her to precede him out of the small private office area. She did so, her eyes darting left and right, looking for escape, something that could be used as a weapon.

''I trust you will be smart enough not to try anything. I would not hesitate to put a bullet in your brain and let you join your father out there in the backyard.''

Bonnie backed up until she stood with her back against the cold Formica countertop of the scientists' worktable. As Jonathon went to a small refrigerator and withdrew a large syringe, her heart banged painfully in her chest, threatening to erupt as black fear swept over her. "You killed my father, didn't you?" she asked, her voice a pale imitation of itself.

"Walter had become a bleeding heart," Jonathon explained in a rational tone that whispered of his complete insanity. "He was old and ill, and his rigid morality restricted the testing of our discovery." He looked at her intently, as if finding it important to make her understand. "We could have gone on testing the drug on monkeys and rats forever, but we needed to see the effects on man. Walter wanted to test and retest, study results. If he'd had his way, we would have never moved forward into an exciting new arena. With the discovery of this new bonding agent, we can learn to take the best traits of animals and combine them with man. Walter's death was a small price to pay for furthering science."

"A small price to pay?" Bonnie stared at him incredulously. "You took a man's life."

Jonathon shrugged. "He was dying, anyway."

"And do you consider what you've done to Nicholas exciting?"

Jonathon grimaced painfully. "My dear, Nicholas has been an enormous disappointment. He should have felt privileged to be a part of this new discovery, but instead he has fought me every step of the way."

"You are a monster," Bonnie exclaimed, anger momentarily overriding her fear. "You're dabbling with things out of the realm of science. Your work is evil. No amount of knowledge is worth destroying lives."

For a moment Jonathon's eyes blazed with the fervent light of a fanatic. "Knowledge is worth any price," he exclaimed. "This is only the beginning. Who knows what direction we'll take from here. If a man can control his DNA, he can control his very destiny. Nicholas is only the beginning. Injecting you is the second phase of the experiment." He advanced toward her, the syringe looking more deadly to Bonnie than the gun he still held in his hand.

"Let her go, Jonathon."

Both Jonathon and Bonnie turned at the sound of Nicholas's deep voice. He stood in the doorway of the lab, looking haggard but determined. His eyes still glowed with the strange silver light, a lingering effect of his recent transformation.

"Ah, Nicholas, I'm afraid I can't do that," Jonathon replied, his tone as pleasant as if he spoke to a dear friend.

Nicholas stepped through the doorway and toward Jonathon, his gaze frighteningly intent as the force of mysterious energy surrounded him. "And I'm afraid that I can't allow you to continue. I will not allow you to infect Bonnie."

"Obviously you've forgotten that I've got a gun," Jonathon countered easily.

"And obviously you've forgotten exactly what I'm capable of," Nicholas returned.

Bonnie watched this exchange, her heart pounding furiously as she felt the danger that surrounded her. It seemed to come to her from all directions. The electricity in the room was suffocating, and she felt it growing like an ominous entity.

Jonathon smiled at Nicholas, a smile of utter confidence. "I don't think you'll chance a transformation with Bonnie right here. There's no guarantee that the beast inside you wouldn't rip her throat out."

It was obvious his words affected Nicholas, who clenched his fists, veins of self-control popping out in his forehead.

"Do it, Nicholas," Bonnie whispered. "Let yourself transform." She spoke with a sudden certainty. "You won't hurt me. He's the beast, not you. Let it happen," she finished passionately. She shoved from her mind the images of the mutilated animals, the havoc in the bedroom he'd destroyed. He had to stop Jonathon. The madman could not be allowed to continue his experiments. He could not be allowed to do these kinds of things to anyone else, and her own safety was unimportant.

Jonathon's burst of laughter turned to a cry of surprise as Nicholas reached out and batted the gun out of his hand. The gun hit the floor and skittered noisily beneath a table on the other side of the room.

For a moment, the room seemed to swell as Bonnie watched Nicholas, his face contorting with the pain and anger that raged within him. Jonathon seemed to shrink as Nicholas grew more formidable. He stared at Jonathon, his eyes deepening their metallic silver hue. "Run, Bonnie...run to the caves," he gasped, his voice raspy and alien. He turned his wolf eyes back on Jonathon. "I'm going to have to kill you," he half growled. Jonathon's blue eyes were no longer cold. They were the eyes of a man looking at death...afraid, horrified, yet cunningly alert.

As Bonnie watched with a mingling of horror and perverse fascination, she saw the man she loved being slowly transformed into a wild beast.

"Bonnie...go!" The words were just barely discernible, and as he turned his back on her, she saw the dark gray fur that crept up the back of his neck.

Without waiting another moment, Bonnie ran.

CHAPTER TWELVE

Bonnie ran up the stairs and headed for the front door. She was just about to open it when somebody touched her on the back. She whirled around, releasing a sigh of relief as she saw Jimmy, a sandwich in one hand, a glass of milk in the other. His red eyebrows danced upward on his forehead quizzically.

"Jimmy, Nicholas and Jonathon are fighting. Nicholas said to go to the caves." She knew she was speaking too fast even as the words tumbled out. Jimmy's expression of perplexity deepened and Bonnie repeated herself, this time slowly and distinctly.

Jimmy's eyes widened and he quickly set his sandwich and glass down. He reached for her hand and grabbed it tightly, then together the two of them left the house.

Outside the night surrounded them, engulfing Bonnie in a world as mysterious and frightening as the scene she'd just fled. Dark clouds skittered across the sky, partially obscuring the moon from view. As the clouds danced onward, blown by phantom winds, Bonnie somehow wasn't surprised to see that the moon was full. It was a werewolf moon, sending down a diffused light that lent to the forest an ominous aura. The night wind rustled the dying leaves on the trees, sounding to Bonnie like skeletal bones in a grave.

She clung to Jimmy's hand tightly, knowing she must be hurting him, but unable to release her death-like grip.

As they plunged into the thick underbrush, heading in the direction of the cave, behind them they heard cries of alarm drifting out of the institute. Bonnie tried to shut them out, not wanting to even imagine what horrors might be taking place.

The forest, with its shadowed tree branches and thorny bushes, was a torment, but she knew it would also provide an effective cover if Jonathon somehow escaped Nicholas's rage and came after her.

On they ran, the sounds coming from the institute no longer audible as they moved deeper and deeper into the dense woods.

Bonnie was completely disoriented and had it not been for Jimmy's lead, she knew she would be hope-lessly lost.

She screamed, pulling Jimmy to an abrupt halt as the bushes next to them suddenly exploded outward. Poised before her in wild, savage splendor was the wolf, his mouth opened to display sharpened fangs of destruction. In an instant, the clouds left the surface of the moon, releasing the full illumination of its roundness, etching the wolf in stark view.

His huge body with its thick fur was powerfully sleek, and Bonnie knew she and Jimmy were in danger...horrible danger. But she couldn't run. She couldn't even move. *This is Nicholas,* her mind screamed. *This is the man you love.* Yet there was no way she could correlate the primitive beast before her with the man who had tenderly rocked her while she'd cried, the man who'd made love to her with magic finesse.

She was vaguely aware of Jimmy grunting, yanking on her hand, then plucking at her arm, trying to make her move, silently begging her to run. But she couldn't. As the wolf growled a menacing sound of warning, her gaze locked with the strange silver eyes.

Time stood still. The forest surrounding her faded away as she fell into the eyes of the wolf. Beneath the wild hunger, beyond the burning rage, she looked deep within the creature and she didn't see the soul of a beast...she saw Nicholas's soul. Her fear fell away from her, like the dying leaves of a tree floating to the ground. She stood before him fearlessly, a sense of inevitability to the confrontation. She was his, to do with as he would.

A moment passed, another moment...a lifetime. Without warning, the wolf raised his head and howled, a lament of anguish that filled the night. Then, gazing at her one last time with his glowing eyes, he turned and disappeared into the darkness.

As if surfacing from a dream, Bonnie once again became aware of Jimmy's panic. Turning to the frightened boy, she gestured for him to continue toward the cave. Hesitating only a moment, looking back at the place where the wolf had disappeared, Bonnie followed Jimmy.

Minutes later she and Jimmy entered the cave. Jimmy reached inside the entrance and withdrew the flashlight, turning it on to light their way through the dark passageway.

Bonnie breathed a sigh of relief as they entered into the larger cavern, the moonlight spilling through the holes of the ceiling and slicing through the utter blackness of the cave.

She sat down on the floor, trying to catch her breath, wondering what had happened to Jonathon, to Mavis and to the other men in the institute. *Nicholas,* her heart cried out, her grief a combination of his pain and the realization that there could never be a future for the two of them. Perhaps it would be best if one time he transformed and never again returned to his human form. Surely it would be better to be a wolf forever than to exist trapped in limbo, between man and beast, never knowing when the wolf might emerge.

She was almost comforted by the thought of Nicholas running free and wild, chasing the moon and living wild, unfettered by human consciousness, guilt and torment. But nothing could ease her own anguish as she contemplated a lifetime without him.

The cavern suddenly filled with light, and she turned to see Jimmy carrying the lantern from Nicholas's little room. He set it down on the cave floor, the light casting deep shadows in the corners. He then sat next to her, touching her arm as if to comfort her.

Bonnie smiled at him, realizing again what a special young man Jimmy was. Despite the fact that he was only sixteen and had to be as scared as her, his first thought was to ease her fear with one of his sunny smiles and a soft touch. *My brother,* she thought, placing her arm around his thin shoulders. He was a part of her father to hold on to, to bond with, and she determined at that moment that no matter what the future held, she would never lose contact with Jimmy.

She didn't now how long they sat there, side by side, waiting for something to happen, some sign that it was safe to return to the institute.

Bonnie turned as she heard a soft, scuffling noise coming from the passageway. She held her breath, waiting to see who—or what—would emerge. Her arm tightened protectively around Jimmy.

"Ah, I knew you'd be here." Jonathon stepped into the cavern, the lantern light gleaming on the gun he held.

Bonnie scrambled to her feet, her heart exploding with renewed fear as she realized she and Jimmy were trapped...trapped with a madman who held a gun. "How...how did you..." She stared at him, observing as if from a great distance the bloody scratch down one side of his face, the rip in one shirtsleeve.

"How did I manage to escape Nicholas?" With one hand, he removed a handkerchief from his pocket and swiped at the blood that ran freely from his facial wound. "My dear, I am nothing if not resourceful." He motioned with the gun for her to sit back down. "And now, we wait. I know sooner or later he'll return here. He'll come back for you, and when he does, it's time for me to abort this particular experiment."

Abort this particular experiment? Bonnie stared at him, realizing he intended to kill both Nicholas and herself. Again her heart banged against her rib cage as fear pumped adrenaline through her. Her gaze darted around the cavern, looking for a route of escape, but there was none.

Jonathon moved closer to where they sat, leaning against one of the cave walls. "I should have followed my instincts and forbade you to come here."

"Why did you finally agree?" Bonnie asked, hoping to keep him talking. Perhaps if Nicholas did come, he would hear Jonathon's voice and be able to do something to save them all.

"I'd seen pictures of you and knew you were an attractive woman. I hoped that Nicholas would be drawn to you." He smiled, looking exceedingly pleased with himself. "And I was right. You and Nicholas surpassed my expectations. It has been most interesting to observe you and Nicholas together." His smile faded and his eyes were cold. "But you, my dear, have become an intolerable nuisance, snooping around and asking questions." He sighed and dabbed at his cheek once again with the handkerchief. "And Nicholas has been an extreme disappointment. He's managed to maintain too much of his humanity and is able to suppress the natural killing instinct even when he's in wolf form."

Bonnie frowned. "But that's not true. What about the animals he killed? The ones Jimmy found in the forest and the ones the sheriff came about?"

Jonathon smiled once again. "Nicholas didn't kill those animals. It did. It was my effort to control him."

"I...I don't understand."

He sighed impatiently, obviously not accustomed to having to spell out his motives for anything. "If Nicholas knew that he'd never hurt anything, anyone, then there would be no reason for him to remain here at the institute. As long as he thought he was a threat to the well-being of others, he was a prisoner of his own conscience. However, he surprised me when he did this to me." Jonathon reached up and touched the ripped skin of his face. "Perhaps there is a latent capacity for violence in him after all."

"Jonathon." Nicholas's voice rang through the cavern as he stepped out of the passageway and into the lantern's glow. Bonnie and Jimmy stood up, Bonnie's gaze focused on the man she loved.

"Nicholas, we've been waiting for you."

"Let them go." Nicholas's attention was focused

intently on Jonathon. To Bonnie he looked like an avenging god of the past, omnipotent, dangerous and without mercy. And Bonnie knew at that moment that Jonathon was wrong. The killing instinct was in Nicholas, as it was in every man if pushed hard enough, long enough. "This is between you and me, Jonathon," he continued. "Let Bonnie and Jimmy go."

"You know I can't do that," Jonathon protested. "She knows too much. She would ruin everything."

"It's all over. Everything is already ruined," Nicholas observed.

"Not so." Jonathon shook his head. "It can still be saved." He looked at Nicholas with detached interest. "It will be interesting to see your reaction when I shoot her. Will the emotional trauma immediately make you transform? And if you do and I kill you...will you be a wolf in death or will you return to your natural form?" His eyes glowed with intense curiosity. "I guess there's only one way to find out." He pointed the gun at Bonnie.

In that single expanded moment in time, Bonnie became aware of several things. She was conscious of Nicholas's cry of impotent rage. She was aware of the moonlight spilling through the hole in the ceiling, bathing her in a golden light that made her a perfect target. And she was somehow reassured by the fact that the last emotion she would carry with her into her death was her love for Nicholas.

She gasped as Jimmy suddenly stepped in front of her, shielding her from Jonathon's deadly intent.

"Get out of the way, boy," Jonathon demanded harshly. "You are expendable as well." He cursed soundly as Jimmy shook his head and stood his ground. "Very well. It will merely take two bullets instead of one."

"I won't let you do that, Jonathon." Mavis stepped out of the deep shadows at the back of the cavern, her hand shaking as it held a gun pointed at the scientist.

"Don't be a fool, Mavis," Jonathon scoffed. "If you get rid of me, where will you go? What will you do? The Redding Institute is the only home you know."

"And Jimmy is the only son I'll have." She moved closer, her hand shaking violently. "You took my soul long ago, but I won't let you hurt my boy."

With a suddenness of movement, Jonathon swung his gun toward the housekeeper. A gunshot resounded, deafening as it echoed its voice of death in the confines of the cave. Jonathon's chest erupted, his shirt blossoming in vivid red. His gun fell from his hand as his eyes widened in surprise. As if in slow motion, he slipped heavily to the floor, his eyes retaining their look of startled surprise.

For a long moment, nobody moved. Only the sound of the gurgling spring lapping at the rocks broke the utter silence. Mavis dropped her gun, the clatter of the metal against the stone floor breaking the stunned inertia.

Nicholas walked over to Jonathon and stared down at him. "He's dead. You shot him right through the heart."

"That's impossible," Mavis said dully, going to Jimmy and placing an arm around him. "That man had no heart."

Bonnie opened her mouth to speak, surprised when the only sound she emitted was a sob. In three strides, Nicholas reached her, enfolding her in his arms, holding her close as she released shivers of shock and the remnants of fear.

"It's over," he whispered into her hair. "It will all be okay now."

But it wasn't over, and she knew the worse was still to come. She still had to tell him goodbye.

"So, what will you do now?" Bonnie asked Nicholas later the next night. The two of them were alone in the study. Mavis and Jimmy had gone up to bed, and the house was silent other than the popping and snapping of the burning logs in the fireplace.

"I'm not sure," he answered softly. He sat in a chair facing the fire, the lines of his face deepened with weariness. Bonnie knew her own face reflected the strain they'd all been under for the past twenty-four hours.

Following Jonathon's death the night before, the

sheriff was called and Mavis was taken to the Hollow Rock jail. She'd been released late in the evening. The death of Jonathon Dennison was ruled self-defense by the sheriff, who didn't seem too upset that the scientist had met a violent end.

The other doctors had disappeared on the night of the full moon. When Nicholas, Bonnie, Jimmy and Mavis had returned from the sheriff's office, the three were gone, along with their clothing.

"I'll remain here and continue to work on an antidote until the pharmaceutical company eventually closes this place down." He turned and looked at her, his gaze caressing her features. "And you'll leave tomorrow and go back to your real life."

Bonnie's heart wrenched at the thought. She walked over to him and knelt on the floor beside his chair. She lay her head on his thigh, feeling the rough texture of his denim jeans beneath her cheek. "I don't want to go," she whispered.

His hand gently stroked her hair, trembling slightly. "I know. I don't want you to go. But we both know this goes beyond our own desires. You must go."

Bonnie nodded, not moving. She wanted to remember the smell of him, the feel of his hand tangling in her hair, the warmth of his body surrounding her.

"Tell me about your life back in New England," he prompted suddenly. "Tell me all the things you do in a day."

"I'll go back to teaching fifth grade in the school

right down the street from the house where I live.''
She closed her eyes, visualizing the way her life had
been before her mother had gotten ill, before she'd
come to this godforsaken place deep in the woods.
''Every morning I'll start my day with two cups of
coffee. If the weather is nice, I'll drink them out on
the back patio, listening to the birds as they chirp
good-morning.''

She spoke for a long time, telling him of her days
at work, the fun of teaching a roomful of bright, rambunctious children, the sense of satisfaction when the
school day was over and she knew she'd connected
with the kids. She told him of her evenings—popping
a dinner into the microwave, occasionally going to a
movie with friends, often going to bed early with a
good book.

What she didn't tell him was that now, when she
awakened first thing in the morning, she would think
of him, wonder about him. She didn't tell him that
now, when she taught her class, she'd mourn for the
man who'd once had a dream of being a teacher. She
didn't tell him that from now on, when she closed her
eyes at night, she would cry, remembering their lovemaking, grieving for the love that had been the victim
of a madman's manipulation.

Instead, she focused on the mundane, everyday
routine of her life, sharing problems with other teachers, tending the garden her mother had planted, work-

ing on a sequined Christmas-tree skirt she'd begun two years before.

She didn't realize she was crying until she finished speaking, licked her lips and tasted the saltiness of her tears.

For a long moment he didn't say anything. His hand moved tenderly through the strands of her hair. "Thank you," he finally said softly. "Now, when you're gone from here and I think of you, I'll be able to picture you in your world instead of in the horror of mine."

Bonnie raised her head and gazed at him, seeing her own torment reflected in his eyes. "No matter where I am, my heart will always be here with you."

He closed his eyes and leaned his head back against the chair, his features reflected starkly in the glow from the fire. "If only your father had written down the antidote. I'm sure he had nearly perfected the formula for one, but I can't find it anywhere."

She stared at him, something in the back of her mind clicking into place. "Nicholas?" He opened his eyes and looked at her. "The letter my father wrote to me...the one in the computer. At the end of the letter, on the last page, were a bunch of symbols and numbers.... You don't suppose..." She didn't finish the sentence as she felt his muscles tighten, saw hope spring into his eyes.

He stood up and pulled her to her feet. Without

another word between them, they hurried downstairs to the lab and the computer.

It took Nicholas only minutes to call up the file, and as he scanned the last page Bonnie could feel his suppressed excitement. "Yes..." he said slowly. "Yes...I think this is it. All the components seem right." He spoke more to himself than to her. "He must have placed it here hoping that Jonathon would never find it."

Hope swelled Bonnie's heart. "Can you duplicate it?" she asked, holding her breath in anticipation.

"Yes...yes, I think I can." He quickly printed out the formula, then Bonnie followed him into the lab, pulling up a stool and watching as he worked to produce the antidote that would make him normal again.

Dawn lit the eastern sky when they finally emerged from the lab, a syringe of the precious fluid in Nicholas's hand. Nicholas had insisted he inject himself while upstairs in his padded room, afraid of what the results would be.

As they stood before the doorway, Nicholas gathered her into his arms, holding her with an intensity that stole her breath away. "Bonnie...I love you. I want you to know that in case anything happens."

Fear swooped down around her as she looked up at him. "What could possibly happen?" she asked.

He released her and held up the syringe, studying the contents solemnly. His gaze turned to her, and for a long moment he merely stared at her. Without saying a word, he stepped into the padded room and closed the door behind him.

He hadn't answered her question and that frightened her. She stared at the closed door, remembering the look on his face as he'd stared at the mixture in the hypodermic needle. She remembered him telling her about when he'd first been injected, how he'd lingered for three days between life and death. She suddenly knew with a gut-wrenching certainty that if the antidote didn't save him, it would kill him.

CHAPTER THIRTEEN

"No." The single word escaped Bonnie, and she realized at that moment that she could love Nicholas without the cure. She'd rather love a beast than risk losing him altogether.

She banged on the door, wanting to stop him, not wanting him to gamble with his life. But her only answer was silence. Running her hands caressingly down the door, she slid to the floor and prepared to wait.

The howling began as dusk slipped fingers of darkness in through the windows. The cries were tortured howls of anguish and pain. Bonnie covered her ears, trying to block out the sounds of torment as tears coursed down her cheeks. She couldn't stand the sound of his pain. She couldn't tolerate the fact that there was nothing she could do to help him through this. He had to endure his hell completely alone.

All through the night, Nicholas's cries rang out, hauntingly forlorn, achingly anguished. At dawn they stopped abruptly, leaving behind a heavy silence that screamed in Bonnie's head. The silence terrified her. She once again placed her palms on the surface of the door, needing to make a connection with him, somehow hoping she would be able to feel his life force radiating within. The door was cold and hard beneath her hands and gave her no hint of what was happening inside the room.

"Nicholas," she whispered softly, not knowing if he was alive or dead. She placed her ear against the door, trying to discern any kind of movement, any sign of life. She gasped in relief as she heard a deep, barely audible moan. With a shuddering sigh, she placed her hands over her face, exhausted by the hours of worry.

"You need some coffee."

She looked up to see Mavis standing in the hallway, a tray in her hand. Bonnie scrambled to her feet, surprised by the woman's unexpected thoughtfulness. "Thanks," she said, taking the coffee and sipping it gratefully.

Mavis looked at the locked door, her eyes darkening in worry. "The devil's work," she whispered, clutching the now empty tray to her chest.

"No...not the devil's work," Bonnie returned tiredly. "Jonathon's madness. Nicholas is merely a victim."

Mavis frowned thoughtfully, then slowly nodded. "I knew Jonathon was evil, but he scared me. He told me nobody would get hurt, that we'd just pretend that he was Walter so they wouldn't close down the institute. I tried to make him stop. I didn't want him hurting you." Mavis reached up and fingered her collar nervously. "Jonathon knew we had no place to go if the Redding Institute closed down. This is the only home Jimmy and I know. I have no money.''

''Weren't you paid for working here?'' Bonnie asked curiously, glancing back at the door to Nicholas's room. She was torn with the need to keep her thoughts firmly focused on him and her curiosity about Mavis and her position here.

Again Mavis clutched the tray tightly against her chest. ''Didn't care much about being paid. Jimmy and I had a place to live, Walter took care of all our needs. Money didn't seem important.'' She looked at Bonnie almost defiantly. ''You know I loved your daddy.''

Bonnie nodded, unable to summon any remaining resentment. In fact, she was grateful her father had had Mavis and Jimmy. And she understood why the older woman had chosen to remain here with Jonathon after Walter's death. She knew no other life. There had been no place else to go. She'd been at the mercy of Jonathon. He'd manipulated her, playing on her helplessness, taking advantage of her as he'd done everyone else. Bonnie couldn't be angry with Mavis, she could only be sad for her. ''What will you do now?''

Mavis sighed, her brow wrinkling once again. ''I don't really know. I suppose we'll pack up and leave here. They won't waste a lot of time in closing this place down now that all the men are gone.''

''Where will you go?'' Bonnie felt a curious

wrench in her heart as she thought of Jimmy, her half
brother, a boy she could easily love.

"Where the wind blows us. I'll look for work,
someplace where I can do what I do best—cook and
clean. Someplace where they won't mind if I have
Jimmy."

"Come to my house," Bonnie said on impulse.
The moment the words of welcome fell from her lips,
she felt the rightness of them. "It's not a mansion,
but it's someplace to stay until you get on your feet."

"Oh, it wouldn't be right." Mavis's protest was
weak, her voice trembling.

"What could be more right?" Bonnie returned vehemently. "Mavis...Jimmy is my half brother.
You're family, the only family I have left. I don't
want to lose touch with him...with you."

Tears misted the older woman's eyes. "I'll think
about it," she said. She looked at the door, the sounds
of Nicholas's moans drifting out to where they stood.
"How much longer can this go on?"

Bonnie shrugged. "He told me that when he was
first injected, for three days he was deathly ill. I suppose the antidote will work in the same kind of time."

Mavis nodded, then turned away and disappeared
back down the stairs.

Bonnie watched her go, somehow certain that when
she left here, she would take a whole new family with
her. She stared at the door that separated her from
Nicholas. Now...if only... She slid back down the

wall, resuming her position of vigilance…hoping… praying.

It was the next day at noon and Bonnie couldn't stand it any longer. There had been not a sound from Nicholas in almost eight hours…no moans, no scuffling, not a single sound indicating life of any kind beyond the door.

She was exhausted, but her exhaustion was nothing next to the fear that rippled in her veins. She couldn't wait another minute. She had to know if he was alive. She stood up and banged on the door with her fists, yelling his name.

"Nicholas…for God's sake," she begged. She pounded on the door until her fists were sore. With a sob of despair, she leaned against the door and heard the audible click of the lock unlatching.

Catching her breath in her lungs, she stepped back, staring intently at the door as it slowly swung inward. Nicholas stood there, looking like a man who'd been to hell and couldn't find his way out. His hair was wildly disarrayed and his body was bathed in a sweat, causing him to shiver uncontrollably. But he was alive…wonderfully still alive.

"Bonnie." Her name was a weak plea for help, and with a sigh, he pitched forward, hitting the floor with a jarring thud.

Bonnie knelt down beside him. She could feel the intense heat that radiated from him and knew he was burning up with an unnatural fever. She gripped him beneath the arms, trying to move him, but he was deadweight, far too heavy for her to move alone.

Minutes later, with the help of Jimmy and Mavis, Nicholas lay unconscious in his bed, Bonnie bathing his face and neck with a cool, damp cloth. His breaths were nearly imperceptible, shallow and faint, and his skin was the white of the sheets of the bed.

"He's not going to make it," Mavis observed from the doorway.

"Yes, he will," Bonnie snapped angrily, then flushed in apology. "He will make it," she exclaimed, returning to her ministrations with a fierce determination. Through sheer willpower alone she would force him to make it through this nightmare.

For two days Nicholas lingered someplace between the land of the living and death. Bonnie bathed his fevered skin, talked to him, loved him. She told him what their life together would be, spinning fantasies of love that made her eyes burn with suppressed tears.

On the second day, he opened his eyes and stared at her, his eyes flickering with the silver hue of the wolf. "Fight it, Nicholas," she whispered. "Damn you, fight it." As she watched, the silver light seemed to flicker, then die. He closed his eyes once again. Minutes later, his fever broke.

"Bonnie…"

She opened her eyes, for a moment disoriented as

she saw the early morning sending shimmering light in through the window. She shifted her position on the chair next to the bed, her bones protesting her awkward sleeping position.

"Bonnie."

She gasped and looked at Nicholas. His eyes were open, the brilliant green of spring. There was no hint of a metallic gleam, and she knew with a certainty in her heart that he'd beaten it. The beast was gone. "Oh, Nicholas!" She flew to the side of the bed, helping him as he struggled to sit up. "How do you feel?" she asked worriedly, relieved to see that his color had returned.

"Weak...but better. Definitely better," he answered, flexing his hands as if testing his strength.

"You beat it, Nicholas. I know you did." She took his hand in hers. "The beast is gone forever. You can leave this place, come home with me. You're finally free."

His eyes darkened slightly and he eased his legs over the side of the bed. "The first thing I need to do is shower, then we'll talk and see where we go from here."

As Nicholas stood beneath the hot spray of the water, he was afraid...afraid that the beast was not gone, as Bonnie had said, but rather hiding deep within him, waiting to spring out unexpectedly.

He'd hoped that by injecting himself with the antidote, all his worries would be over, he would finally be able to return to a normal life. He hadn't anticipated the fear, and he hadn't anticipated his enormous love for Bonnie.

There was no way he could make a life with her, no way he could put her through the worry of waiting...anticipating that each time he lost his temper he would transform into a beast that might harm her. He couldn't live like that. He wouldn't live like that. Decision made, he finished his shower, then went out to talk to Bonnie.

As he walked into the study, he saw her standing in front of the window, the morning light caressing her in glorious golden hues. For a moment she didn't seem to feel his presence behind her, and he merely stood silently and drank in her beauty, knowing thoughts of her would somehow bring him comfort as he lived his solitary life.

She turned suddenly, her eyes lighting up as she saw him. She arose and came to him, immediately wrapping her arms around his waist and leaning her head against his chest.

He stiffened, needing distance to do what had to be done. Gently he disentangled her and stepped back. "Bonnie, we need to talk." He watched the play of emotions on her face, the smile fading as worry darkened the green of her eyes. She embodied all that he'd ever dreamed of. She was home, she was contentment...she was love. And he knew to save them both he had to let her go.

He motioned for her to sit down and he eased himself into the chair across from her, knowing he had to let her go, but unsure where to begin. "Bonnie." Even her name hurt as it fell from his lips, and he anticipated the pain to come. "Bonnie, we've been living a fool's fantasy, pinning too much hope on an antidote we're not even sure worked."

"It worked," she replied serenely.

"We can't know that," he countered.

"I know it worked. I know it here." She touched her heart with the tip of her index finger.

Nicholas stood up, running a hand through his hair. "Bonnie, how can you be so certain? I don't know if I'm cured. It may take months, years, before I feel that the antidote worked, before I know that the effects of the bonding agent are gone." His voice lowered. "I won't leave here until I'm sure. I won't risk hurting anyone."

"But *I'm* sure." Again her voice was soft with conviction. "I saw the beast leave you, I saw the glow leave your eyes. It's gone, Nicholas. It's truly gone."

"Dammit, Bonnie!" Nicholas's anger exploded out of him…anger at her for making this difficult, anger at Jonathon for his madness, and anger at himself for wanting so desperately what Bonnie offered him. "Don't fight me on this. Don't make it any more difficult than it already is." He paced back and forth in front of her. "You will leave here tomorrow. You'll get on with your life. You'll find a normal man, a man who you won't have to fear each time he gets angry."

"I've already found the man I want to spend the rest of my life with, and I'm not leaving here without you."

Suddenly a rage was upon Nicholas, a rage that had its source in the unfairness of their situation, a rage that had been building in him since the moment he'd experienced his first transformation. He felt it building inside, so enormous, so intense he had no time to control it. It washed over him and he rode with it, unable to do anything else.

Cursing violently, he stared at Bonnie in horror. "Get out of here, Bonnie." He clenched his fists, feeling the hated familiar heat uncoiling in his stomach. The antidote hadn't worked. His body filled with heat. "Bonnie, for the love of God, run."

Her eyes widened slightly, but she merely shook her head, not moving from her chair and further increasing his torment. Through his red mist of anger, he realized he had to get away from her. He started for the door, surprised when she jumped out of her chair and blocked his escape. "Dammit, Bonnie, get out of my way," he shouted.

"I'm not running, and neither are you," she said softly, her eyes fearless as she gazed up at him.

"Can't you feel it?" he asked, every muscle tense as he waited for the change to sweep him into the darkness of hell. "Can't you see that the antidote didn't work, that it's going to happen again and I can't stop it?''

She reached up and touched the side of his face, her light caress an aching addition to the pain that sliced through his temples. "It's all right, Nicholas."

He stumbled away from her, not wanting to be anywhere near her when his hands turned to claws, his teeth lengthened to sharp canines. "Dear God, I'm out of control," he whispered in anguish.

"Nothing is going to happen," Bonnie answered, knowing she was right. The force, the energy that she'd always noticed before a transformation, was absent. There was no metallic glimmer in his eyes... only the dark pain of an angry man.

He covered his face with his hands, his body almost vibrating with tension. A minute passed, then another and another. As Bonnie watched, he slowly removed his hands, a look of bewilderment on his face.

She reached out and touched his arm, feeling the tension ebbing, retreating from him. "Nicholas...it's anger, good, old-fashioned, healthy anger."

"Yes...yes, I'm angry, but I'm not changing." He looked at his hands, as if unable to believe that they were only hands. He gripped them tightly closed, watching as his knuckles turned white. He looked back at her, his eyes filling with tears, but for the first time full of tentative hope. "Do you really think it's gone?"

Bonnie moved into his arms and gazed deep into

his eyes, seeing only the soul of the man she loved. "Yes, Nicholas. You're free."

He smiled, the first genuine one she'd ever seen, and the beauty of it made her heart skip a beat. *"Free."* He repeated the word, savoring it on his lips. "Oh, yes. I'm free." He closed his eyes and leaned his head back, as if contemplating the very essence of his freedom.

"Nicholas, will you leave here with me?"

He opened his eyes and looked at her, pulling her closer into his embrace. "Will I leave here with you?" He laughed, the rich, deep sound Bonnie had heard him share only with Jimmy. The melodious tones rolled over her, through her, stroking the love she had for him to a fever. "I can't think of anything I would rather do." His eyes were warm, caressing as he gazed at her. "Bonnie, I want to share coffee with you in the mornings. I want to fall asleep with you in my arms. I want to live in that world you painted for me with your words."

Bonnie blinked back her tears, feeling one errant teardrop escape and run down her cheek. He took his finger and gently swiped it away. "Our tears are over," he said softly. "Will you marry me and share your life with me?"

"Yes, oh yes," she whispered, her heart so full.

He claimed her lips in a kiss that held all his unfulfilled dreams, all his aching loneliness, and she took them and replaced them with all the love she had inside her. When he finally broke the kiss, his eyes glowed, not with the light of a werewolf, but this time with the inner illumination of a man in love. Bonnie felt herself bathed in the light, and she knew that it was worth the risk of braving the beast to discover the man within. She'd found the heart of the beast and claimed it for her own.

EPILOGUE

The dining room looked splendid. The table was set with their best china, and candles glowed next to the floral centerpiece. Nicholas stood in the doorway, looking around the room with a sense of contentment that had only grown in the past two years.

Two years. It seemed impossible to believe. The days at the institute seemed like a lifetime ago. Bonnie had filled up his life so totally he rarely thought of the hell he'd endured.

He walked over to the window and peered out into the darkness. There were times when he closed his eyes, that he thought he could remember running fast in the moonlight, feeling the cool night breeze caressing him. The half-remembered sensation always brought with it a profound sense of loneliness, an ache in his chest that nothing could assuage. Nothing except...

"Nicholas?"

He turned at the sound of her voice, as always the strange emptiness filled by her mere presence. "There's my girls," he said, moving across the room to her. He placed one arm around her back, and with the other he patted her very pregnant stomach. "How's my little one doing this evening?"

"She's being most rambunctious, all elbows and knees," Bonnie replied with a small smile. "I think she must know this is a very special night for her mother and father."

"Hmm." He leaned down and kissed Bonnie, his hand still caressing her round belly. They knew the baby was a girl because he had insisted on every test possible to make certain the baby was normal. "Out of all the things I've done in my life…this is my very best accomplishment," he said softly.

"Unfortunately, you can't take all the credit," Bonnie teased him, her smile turning wistful. "My father said much the same thing in the letter he left for me. I'm so pleased they are naming the new institute after him." She reached up and caressed Nicholas's face. "And I'm thrilled that they had the good judgment to name you head of the teaching staff."

"And I hope that I can make sure that all the young scientists who come there to school are taught the right things…ethics, morality and humanity."

"You'll do wonderfully," she replied without doubt.

"You two had better quit your cuddling. Your first guests just pulled up in the driveway," Mavis exclaimed as she carried a plate of hors d'oeuvres to the coffee table.

A half hour later, Bonnie sat at the table, surrounded by friends who'd all come to celebrate Nicholas's appointment to the Redding School of Science.

She looked down toward the head of the table where Nicholas sat laughing and socializing with her best friend, Susan.

There were times when she thought she was living a dream and prayed she would never awaken. Her life was so full of love.

After leaving the institute two years earlier, they had come back here, to the home where Bonnie had lived with her mother. Mavis and Jimmy had come with them. They had served as witnesses at Bonnie and Nicholas's courthouse wedding.

They had to return to Hollow Rock only once, for the inquest into Jonathon's death. Mavis was duly exonerated of any wrongdoing, and once again they had all returned here.

In the first couple of weeks Mavis had talked about getting a job, but she quickly made herself indispensable in the household. Now, with the baby nearly due, she'd stopped talking about getting another job, and Bonnie was grateful for the woman's friendship.

Jimmy attended a special school for the hearing impaired, and he had blossomed in the atmosphere of acceptance. He was becoming a typical eighteen-year-old, anxious to be on his own, just beginning to realize his own potential.

Days would pass when Bonnie didn't even think about the horrors they had all endured in the house buried in the woods of the Ozarks. And each day, she saw Nicholas release more of his painful memories.

She now looked down the table at the man who had captured her heart so completely. She smiled and blushed as his eyes locked with hers, speaking hotly, intimately in the language of love.

"You two had better stop looking at each other that way or the rest of us will feel compelled to leave you alone," Susan observed with a wry grin.

"Would you mind?" Nicholas teased.

Susan laughed and tapped him lightly on the shoulder. "Honestly, Nicholas, you're irrepressible." She smiled at Bonnie. "How could you ever marry such a beast?"

"If you think I'm a beast now, you should have seen me when we first met," Nicholas replied, his eyes dark and sensual. He looked back at Bonnie and smiled, a smile that held a future of secrets shared, sorrows eased, enduring passion and love forever. Bonnie returned his smile, rubbing her stomach as Nicholas's child kicked an unspoken sign of happiness.

* * * * *

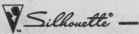

In October 2001 look for

A FATHER'S VOW
by Tina Leonard

Lost

One twin. Ben Mulholland
desperately needs a bone marrow
donor to save his little girl, Lucy.
The brother Ben never knew he
had is her best, maybe only, chance.
If he can just track him down…

Found

The miracle of hope. Caroline St. Clair
has loved Ben forever and she'll do
whatever it takes to ensure he doesn't lose his precious
daughter. In the process, old wounds are healed and flames
of passion reignited. But the future is far from secure.

Finders Keepers: bringing families together

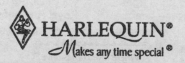

Conveniently Yours

THE BRAVO BILLIONAIRE

As a child, Jonas Bravo saw his baby brother kidnapped before his very eyes—and life, as he knew it, would never be the same. Now, with another child's well-being at stake, he was determined to fight the good fight. But to hold on to *this* baby, he would have to marry her guardian. And though he didn't trust her as far as he could throw her, Jonas knew he had to let lovely Emma Hewitt into his life. For was it possible that this woman, and this child, were about to bring back everything he'd lost that long-ago winter night...and thought he would never see again?

THE BRAVO BILLIONAIRE, by Christine Rimmer:
On sale in September 2001, only from Silhouette.

And coming in October, the missing Bravo baby is
alive and well...and all grown up. Find him in
THE MARRIAGE CONSPIRACY by **Christine Rimmer**
(SE #1423)—on sale in October 2001,
only from Silhouette Special Edition.

Available wherever Silhouette books are sold.

Silhouette®
Where love comes alive™

In September 2001,

V *Silhouette*

SPECIAL EDITION™

presents the final book in

DIANA PALMER's

exciting new *Soldiers of Fortune* trilogy:

THE LAST MERCENARY

(SE #1417)

Traveling far and wide to rescue Callie Kirby from a dangerous desperado was far less daunting for Micah Steele than trying to combat his potent desire for the virginal beauty. For the heavenly taste of Callie's sweetly tempting lips was slowly driving Micah insane. Was the last mercenary *finally* ready to claim his bride?

Don't miss any of the adventurous
SOLDIERS OF FORTUNE *tales from*
international bestselling author Diana Palmer!

MERCENARY'S WOMAN, SR #1444
THE WINTER SOLDIER, SD #1351
THE LAST MERCENARY, SE #1417

Soldiers of Fortune...prisoners of love.

Available only from Silhouette Books at your favorite retail outlet.

V *Silhouette*®
Where love comes alive™